Girl, 1983

# Girl, 1983
*Linn Ullmann*

Translated from the Norwegian by Martin Aitken

W. W. NORTON & COMPANY
*Independent Publishers Since 1923*

copyright © TK

I

Blue

I'm sixteen years old and fold my arms on the tall table in front of me, rest my cheek against one arm and look into the camera. The photograph, which no longer exists and which no one apart from me remembers, hints at my bare shoulders. I think the idea is to suggest nakedness, that all a young woman needs to wear when setting out in the world is a pair of long earrings.

I didn't think you existed any more, only then you turned up under an elm tree in September a year and a half ago, demanding to be heard.

You're transparent. Almost without features. Watery.

Things I know about you:

Our mother gave birth to you while asleep, and then you ran away.

You ask me to do impossible things and never listen when I say I can't.

Describing you is one of the hardest things I've had to do.

Sometimes I think our mother suspects I'm not the only one, that there are two of us, but then she blots it out. *Not now!*

Elm seeds descend on Oslo this spring, twirling to the ground day after day, the gentlest of storms, silent, like autumn leaves or dirty snow they pile up along the pavements and in the parks, whirling across the rooftops. I search the Internet wondering if it's a good or bad sign, *what does it mean*, there are so many of them. *Is* it a sign? I think I probably attach too much importance to signs, or what I take to be signs. Elm seeds are drifting into people's apartments, thin, flaky seeds that don't look like seeds at all, scribbling patterns in the air. They come to rest on the floor, in the bathtub, on the bed sheets. I type *large amounts of elm seeds*, which elicits nothing. I type *elm seeds sign* and draw a blank with that too.

*Lie still*, you said, caringly almost, *let me hold you*. I tried to get up, it was morning, I heard Eva's voice in the living room, my husband said something that made her laugh, but you said *no*. So, I stayed in bed, listening to a podcast interview with the American poet Sharon Olds, whose poetry I'd translated, just for myself, and just a few pieces. Olds said the reason she no longer wears make-up is to scare people. If they're close enough, she said, they can see something is different about me, something unnerving. I am embryonic, she said (and I was reminded of you then), pre-eyebrows, pre-eyelids, pre-mouth.

I, on the other hand, have all those things (eyebrows, eyelids, mouth), and the story I want to tell begins with a photograph taken by K in a studio in Paris in winter 1983. The long earrings were made of rhinestone, they weren't expensive at all, I had a box full of similar trinkets in my room in the apartment I shared with my mother in New York. Dangly earrings. Glittery earrings. Rhinestones were all the rage. But one of the gems, the one nearest the earlobe, was blue, I remember that.

~

Or perhaps the story begins a few months earlier, in late autumn. I'm a junior in high school, but rarely show up for class. The new coat, bought at Bloomingdale's in early January, is full-length and made of blue wool with a tie-belt at the waist. I'm sixteen years old. K lives in New York but keeps an apartment in Paris. Maybe you'd like to go with me some time, he says.

~

When I was six or seven, and again when I was eleven, and again when I was thirteen, I dreamed of big blue jellyfish with long tentacles. Everything in the dream was blue. My lips, from the cold water; the clouds, the sea. I read somewhere (after I grew up and no longer dreamed about them) that jellyfish go through various life cycles. Larva, polyp, medusa. I wasn't scared. Not in the dream.

~

I'm sixteen years old. It's the middle of the night. I'm in K's apartment in Paris, still wearing my coat. It's a small apartment, a combined living room and kitchen, wood floors and tall windows, a bathroom with blue tiles above the sink. I've positioned myself in the middle of the room. I've wrapped my arms around my waist in a kind of embrace, or as if they were an extra belt to keep my coat in place.

Aren't you going to take your coat off?
Yes, sure.
It's very late.
Yes.
Why did you come here?
What do you mean?
I mean, instead of going to your hotel?

~

You're the girl who will not die, and now, after having been gone for years, you've woven yourself back inside of me. When I was little, I imagined you lived either in the wallpaper or within my clothes, and that you looked like a big insect, a dragonfly, and that instead of a dress you had a double set of shimmering wings.

I imagined that we were sisters. I had four half-sisters, but missed having a *whole* sister, a *real* sister, one who was *always* there. I had my best friend, Heidi, who was my mirror image, but Heidi already had a sister. You and I promised we'd never leave each other. I wanted us to take a blood oath to seal the promise, but you weren't made of blood, so we didn't.

When I was little, I was afraid of insects and of the dark and of grown-ups who drank themselves into a stupor —
    and of nuclear war and of my parents' rage —
    and of death, not my own, but Mamma's —
    and of ball games and of loud noises —
    and of being tightly held —

~

The first time I met K was in October 1982 in an elevator ascending the grand old building between West 56th and West 57th Street. We didn't speak then, so perhaps *met* isn't the right word. Forty years later, I picture a crammed elevator stopping on every floor, people coming and going. Later, when we got to know each other, he told me he fell in love with my smile. It wasn't true, it was just something he said. At sixteen I wasn't in the habit of smiling. Perhaps he fell in love with the pink-and-white striped dress I had on, part candy cane, part punk, and my big red woolly hat. I don't mean the dress as such — sleeveless, strappy, snug around my breasts and waist, flaring into a soft knee-length skirt — but the girl who so obviously loved showing herself off in it. The narrow waist isn't new, she's always been thin, the breasts are more recent and not yet fully developed. She was flat as an ironing board until the year turned from 1981 to 1982. Her borrowed, open leather jacket is four sizes too big over her bare shoulders, in stark contrast to the pink-and-white striped summer dress beneath; the only function the leather jacket has in this scene is to be removed, for someone to snatch it from her frame.

According to a study about what makes up the human body, the brain and the heart are composed of 73% water, the lungs of 83% water, the skin of 64% water, the muscles and the kidneys of 79% water and the skeleton of 31% water. The events I'm relating here, what happened before, during and after K took a photograph of me in Paris, are made up mostly of forgetting, just as the body is composed mostly of water. The parts I can't remember – perceptible only as dreams and sensations – seem to me unwritable, but I'm determined to write them down anyway.

~

K stepped out of the elevator, went down the long corridor, unlocked the door to his studio, picked up the phone and called the woman I'll refer to as Maxine, whose office was in the same building. *I saw a girl just now in the elevator. Is she one of yours?*

I'm trying to remember K's voice, and Maxine's, and the sixteen-year-old Norwegian girl's. She speaks more English than Norwegian, now that she's moved with her actress mother to New York. I've no recollection of that voice. English is neither her mother's nor her father's language, she herself is half Norwegian, half Swedish, and I imagine a hint of cheek in the way she talks that has to do with her English, as if this third language were a borrowed dress she pretends is her own, and I hear an uncertainty too – the girl is uncertain about everything – and this uncertainty without doubt lends her voice an inflection her Swedish father, if he'd heard her, would have dismissed as *förljugenhet*, affectation.

I've looked for K and Maxine on the Internet, searched for video and audio, but found nothing. I thought maybe if I heard their voices, *our* voices, it might jog my memory.

*Send her upstairs to me, I'd like to take a look.*

Maxine dressed stylishly in loose-fitting black robes that seemed to cover every inch of her skin. She wore long white pearl necklaces and big round spectacles with black frames. Beauty is many things, she would say. She started out as an agent for promising photographers, then after a while went on to represent a diverse selection of models: girls and boys, black and white, straight and gay, young and not so young. She was ahead of her time, envisaging a world where girls and boys, black and white, straight and gay, were no longer stable categories. I have a small picture of her in my desk drawer. Maxine has her hair up, a thin belt around her waist and a silver brooch fastened over her left breast. She's younger in the photograph than when I knew her. She's with a woman in a dark suit and tie, they're arm in arm, standing stiffly side by side like an old married couple, posing, messing around and having fun.

She was right, Maxine, about beauty being many things, and she said so in an age when *beautiful* was synonymous with white, thin, tall, blue-eyed. I'm referring specifically to girls – girls and their beauty – not to other things that are beautiful, like vases, trees, roses, stones. I spent a lot of time on *beautiful*. Was I beautiful? No. But your mother is one of the most beautiful women in the world, Maxine said, and she was right about that, of course.

Maybe I can make something of you, she said.

Two years later, in 1984, Marguerite Duras published her novel *The Lover*, in which she wrote: *What I want to seem I do seem, beautiful too, if that's what people want me to be.* And now K had called and said he'd like to *take a look*.

I'd lose the leather jacket, Maxine said. Don't hide your figure.

It's not mine, I said, I've borrowed it.

I don't care, she said. Take it off. K works for French *Vogue*. He's one of the best. He saw you, and maybe now he'll use you.

*He saw me in the elevator.*

He said I smiled at him, but it's not true. What I did when I sensed he was looking at me was to straighten my posture, roll my shoulders back – a flex – a simple piece of choreography for a sixteen-year-old girl who's done with being a child, a tiny movement that runs through the hips, the spine, the neck, the cheeks, the brow, and then he called Maxine and said he'd like to take a look.

\*

I took off my leather jacket but kept Mamma's red woolly hat on. My arms were cold.

Goosebumps, he said when he opened the door and let me in.

He indicated my bare arms.

Because it's October, I said, almost November.

How old are you – fourteen, fifteen?

Sixteen.

~

Just before Christmas, K invites me over for a drink at his place. He lives and works in the same building. There are some other people there, a small gathering, no dinner, just blue drinks and cocaine. The apartment is spacious and uncluttered, with great arching windows, bookshelves, and photographs on the walls. I like K's white walls and the way all the photographs are mounted in simple black frames. On this particular evening not long before Christmas, he and I sit on the light wood floor, each holding a glass with something blue in it. Someone has put on a record. Jimi Hendrix. K tucks a strand of hair behind my ear and tells me I should cut it short like Mia Farrow –

In *Rosemary's Baby*, I interject.

Exactly, he says, like Mia Farrow in *Rosemary's Baby* . . . and then he breathes the words *her father's daughter* in my ear. Many of the men in his family have worked in film, so we have that in common.

A tall, sylphlike woman trips over our feet in passing and lies there unable to get up. I wonder if tucking a strand of hair away from a girl's face counts as a caress. Isn't he too old to want me in that way?


For someone who's only fifteen, this kid has seen a lot of movies, K says to the woman as she eventually gets to her feet and staggers towards the bathroom. He points at me. *Her father's daughter*, he says again. The sylphlike woman shakes her head.
I really don't give a fuck, she mutters.
K looks at me and laughs.
I'm nobody's daughter, I say.
He nods.
Okay.
I'm sixteen and nobody's daughter.
He lights a cigarette. Offers me one. I take it.
Paris, he says. In January. Are we on?


~


You're not going, Mamma says. Absolutely not. I won't allow it. It's one hundred per cent inappropriate. And anyway, you've got school, you can't just . . . *you can't just go to Paris!*
Mamma doesn't know that I hardly ever go to

school, that the teachers wouldn't know the difference if I was in Paris, New York or anywhere else. My teachers have written letters, my absence is a problem, a cause for concern, but in each case I made them disappear before Mamma got a chance to read them, forging her signature on the form that has to be returned to confirm receipt.

You're too young to travel by yourself, Mamma says. You're too young to be on your own.

I'm not.

I don't know how many ways I can say it, she says, and looks at her hands as if to count her fingers to determine exactly how many ways she can say no.

I roll my eyes.

You don't get it, I say. He works for French *Vogue*. He wants to work with me. He wants to –

I really can't stand it when you roll your eyes like that, Mamma interrupts, her voice bordering on shrill. By the time one turns fourteen, rolling the eyes is completely unacceptable.

What?

I said, by the time one turns fourteen, rolling the eyes is completely unacceptable!

Is that a *rule*?

It's a saying, she says. It's something we say in our family.

But it's completely acceptable to deny one's daughter the chance of being happy, I shout. Is that a saying too? In *our* family?

~

I was fourteen, fifteen, sixteen, and drank until I threw up or fell asleep. I woke in the morning and couldn't remember where I'd been or what had happened the night before. I quit drinking heavily when I was nineteen, but the forgetting – the blacking out – has followed me my whole life.


*Blackout* is the wrong word. The kind of forgetting I'm thinking about isn't black but white.


Anne Carson writes about untranslatable words – words we can say out loud, though without being able to define, possess or make use of them: *Almost as if you were presented with a portrait of some person – not a famous person but someone you might recognize if you put your mind to it – and as you peer closely you see, in the place where the face should be, a splash of white paint.*


When I get to the words *a splash of white paint*, I think of my face when I was sixteen and I was introduced to K.

~

When I moved to New York with Mamma, I enrolled at a high school on West 61st Street and signed up for French 2, which suggests I'd already taken and passed French 1, but when I got to Paris in January 1983, I couldn't understand a word anyone was saying, let alone make myself understood. Either I'd forgotten everything I'd learned, or else I'd never learned anything in the first place.

I was away from school for most of 1982. Days, weeks. I'd go to the movies in the afternoon, sip black coffee on broken benches in Central Park and spend hours at the Museum of Natural History. At the museum, I was drawn to small things. I'd move straight past the great blue whale (ten thousand kilos of foam and fibreglass suspended from the ceiling) in search of miniatures. *I am like a water bear*, Sharon Olds said in the podcast the morning I was reminded of you and of the days alone at the museum almost forty years ago. Water bears are everywhere – in the sea, in glaciers, in leaf litter and mosses, they're in the park across the street from where I live now. When necessary – when they must – they turn themselves into little barrels. They can withstand anything. Extreme heat. Extreme cold. Radioactive disasters. Space travel.

I'm sixteen. I go to the movies, sip black coffee on benches in the park and spend hours alone at the museum.

~

But why did you go to Paris? What were you hoping to find?

The sixteen-year-old girl looks at me with defiance.

How am I supposed to answer that?

And then:

I'm not a kid any more, she says.

I want to be the object, the centre, the focus of another's desire.

I don't want to be alone.

~

I haven't held on to many things from that time. I kept a diary in the years before I turned fifteen and resumed when I was eighteen, but in the three years in between I didn't write anything. The photograph K took of me wearing the earrings is gone, but there's another image from 1983 still in existence. I remember that the photographer – the woman who took this other picture – was French but spoke English fluently. I remember she was elegant. Maybe I told her I was just back from Paris.

It's still winter. We're walking down Columbus Avenue, we find a café, we look at each other over coffee, talking (almost like girlfriends), when she takes out her camera and starts taking pictures.

The thing with K isn't over yet, he calls me day and night, asks me to come over, but I don't tell the woman photographer any of that.

In the picture she took of me, I'm wearing a blue sweater, looking straight at the camera.

Another thing unearthed from 1983 is a letter from my French teacher. I can think of no reason why I should have kept it. It turned up in a cardboard box in the attic, a box with *New York* scribbled on top, and hardly anything in it. The letter from my French teacher isn't very long, it's more of a warning than a letter, of what will happen if my poor attendance continues. It appears from the letter that the French teacher's name is Monsieur O. I have no recollection of him, none whatsoever, it's difficult to fathom that we've ever had anything to do with each other. Not even when I find a picture of him in the school yearbook – the one from 1984, the year after I went to Paris – do I recognize or even vaguely remember him.

*

Because I'm a senior in 1984 there's a picture of me in that yearbook too. I'm wearing heavy make-up, a black turtleneck and black jeans, my face of the previous year, when I was sixteen, now gone completely. I've got strawberry-blonde, shoulder-length hair and look like a different girl altogether.

I leaf back to the picture of Monsieur O. I wait for something to happen. For something to slot into place in my brain. *Oh yes, now I remember.* How come such a moment never occurs? I look at the picture and instead of remembering, all I do is continue to forget.

Is this K's experience too?
    If presented with a photograph of me, even one he took himself, would he shake his head and say, No, I don't remember her, sorry, I don't know what else to say?

In 1984, Monsieur O was a man with a great big mane of grey hair, dreaming of an entirely different life. I don't know that, of course. I'm making it up. Maybe he loved being a French teacher at a West Side high school in New York in the early eighties. In the picture he's smiling. He's wearing a white shirt, a tweed jacket and a wide tie. He's hunched over a big white electric typewriter, and in the background I glimpse a white bookcase and stacks of paper. Are they manuscripts? Is Monsieur O working on a novel? None of the other teachers have been photographed with a typewriter, bookcase and stacks of paper. Several have been photographed in classrooms, in front of a blackboard, for instance, or in the staffroom, or in one of the corridors.

I flip through the yearbook pages.

Some of the teachers I remember clearly – the maths teacher, Mr C; the English teacher, Dr L; and the physics teacher, Mrs T, posing in a white lab coat in front of the periodic table.

I turn back to the picture of Monsieur O. I imagine he and the photographer have agreed in advance on what kind of picture they want: Monsieur O will be seated at his typewriter, in a room suggestive of great things happening in it (the manuscripts), and just as the photographer enters the room, Monsieur O will look up, as if caught off guard.

What I remember is –

What I remember is: I was lost. I didn't know anything about Paris. I couldn't find my way. This is what happened. I wasn't prepared, I just got up and left in a new blue coat and knee-high boots.

*

In New York, the city where I lived with my mother, I knew my way. If you happened to meet that sixteen-year-old girl in New York sometime in the early eighties, you might have asked her for directions and in all likelihood she'd have been able to give them. But – and I was aware of this: New York wasn't the girl's city, even if she lived there. I don't know if she had a city. Or even a place. For a long time – perhaps right until she went to Paris to be photographed by K – her mother was the closest she had to a place. Wherever her mother was, that's where she'd want to be. She longed for her mother's laughter. Her voice. Her scent.

And then there was you. My invisible sister. When I was too old to have invisible sisters, you came back as something else. Formless, nameless. A spiral of restlessness, forgetfulness and unfinished stories. *I'll never leave you again.* Were we together in Paris? Were we one or two? *You, you, you.* Half insect, half ghost. You came in September and grew wildly. You wound yourself around me and inside me, until it was impossible to tell where you began and I ended, which of us was which.

~

It's night. I'm wearing a dress I've borrowed from another girl – a thin blue silky thing that just about reaches my thighs – and the blue coat Mamma and I bought before I left. It keeps me warm. I can't speak French, other than the odd word. I'm wearing Mamma's red woolly hat too. An old couple comes towards me on the pavement, I see them clearly (even now, nearly forty years on) in the light of the street lamps. They look kind; the woman has long dark hair and a red hat like mine. A huge white dog walks between them. They can help me. Yes, they can. I go towards them. I stop in front of them and stand in such a way that they can't possibly go past and continue their evening walk with their dog without speaking to me first – or rather, not their evening walk but their middle-of-the-night stroll, because it's the middle of the night now – I bring them to a halt there on the pavement underneath a street lamp, and ask for their help. I need to find my hotel. I can't remember the address. I was supposed to be back in my room hours ago. To take my mother's phone call at 10 p.m. It was the only way she would let me go. I say all of this in English. I wave and gesticulate, as if arms and hands can put across what language can't. Arms and hands are sometimes sufficient when language falls short, for example when dancing, making love, fighting, or playing an instrument, or if you happen to be a cardiologist performing heart surgery. But not in this instance. Clearly not. I stand on the pavement, I won't let them pass, I wave and gesticulate. Help me find my way, please. I have a room in a hotel. I don't know where it is, but behind the reception desk there's a key that's mine. My mother's been calling all night. She's scared. She's angry.

The couple gawp at me. They shake their heads and shrug their shoulders. I'm sorry, says the woman in the red hat like mine, I'm sorry, she says again, and with a dainty, blue-gloved hand waves me aside, obliging me to make way, so that she and the dog and her husband may continue on.

What I remember is —

What I remember is the first morning in Paris — before I got lost — and the white light in the large, bunker-like studio. The girls taking their seats, one after another, each perching on a high stool in a beam of light waiting for K to photograph them. The floor-to-ceiling mirrors in the make-up area are edged with light bulbs. Music is throbbing in the background, Hall & Oates, *she's a maneater*, which apparently isn't about a dangerous woman at all, as I thought then, as everybody thought — all it takes is a few chords before we start carefully swaying our slender hips there in the studio, exactly as we've done a hundred times before alone in our bedrooms — a dangerous woman with a string of men in her wake, men driven crazy by desire and longing. To have such power. Such a body. To awaken such desire. In 2014, as I sit down (yet again) to write about the girl from 1983, only to give up shortly after, the *Philadelphia Inquirer* publishes an interview with John Oates in which he explains that 'Maneater' isn't about a woman at all, but about New York City in the eighties: about greed, desire and broken dreams.

I remember putting on long rhinestone earrings.

What I *don't* remember is: my French teacher, Monsieur O. He's disappeared from my recollections. I wonder if he shrugs (like the couple with the dog) when once in a blue moon he sees me in the school corridors. *There's that girl who never comes to class.* I lean forward to study his picture. He looks like a man who shrugs often.

In his letter of concern to Mamma – typewritten, probably on the big white typewriter – he has taken great pains to be exact, describing his habitually absent sixteen-year-old student as precisely as he can: *If only your daughter was more prepared, more conscientious in planning her days, not only would her performance markedly improve, she would also be a calmer person. At present she must endure the stress of forever having to work under the pressure of short deadlines. Being better prepared would, I am certain, lessen her anxiety a great deal.*

~

It's spring. The dog and I walk in the park. He doesn't like that I talk on the phone when we go for walks, he asks that my attention not be divided between too many things at once, but he puts up with it, the walks, the phone, the way he puts up with most things, come to think of it, his own ageing, his limp, his plodding pace, his forlornness whenever he's taken for granted. He forgives, always.


My mother and I talk about alcohol.

I *wanted* to black out, she tells me on the phone. She hasn't had a drink in thirty years.

I drank, she says, because I didn't want to be where I was. I wanted to sleep. To disappear.

Disappear?

I don't mean *disappear* disappear, she says. Not for good, just for a while. A break.

She asks how I managed to hide my drinking from her.

It wasn't that hard, I tell her. Mamma laughs, uneasily.

And so I laugh too.


~


The next day, Eva says: I saw a girl.

What girl? Where?

On the Internet, she says, a new platform where students can log on and do homework together. From all over the word. It's a lockdown thing.

Okay, I say. So, what happens? What's the point of it?

Nothing happens, she says, I think that *is* the point. You can't hook up or send messages or anything like that – it's muted, microphones not an option, all completely without sound, like the study area in the school library, except they're never quiet even if they're meant to be. But here – it's silent. You can't hear anyone, you can't hear anything. You just log on and do your homework, or stare into space or into the camera, I saw someone playing the guitar, but couldn't hear it.

The dog lumbers along between Eva and me, dictating the pace, slowly because he's old, first through Torshovparken, then on to the second park with the almost identical name, Torshovdalen – *the park* and *the valley* for short – round and round the large doll's head cast in bronze.

Mamma, Eva says, do you remember the first lockdown, when we dressed up just to go to the doll's head and back?

I nod.

I want to know more about the girl on the Internet. Where's she from?

I've no idea, says Eva, she's likely to be in the same time zone as me, although not necessarily – a lot of people log on in the middle of the night, but there's something daylike about her.

What do you mean, daylike?

I don't know – like she got up at dawn or something.

I ask what it was exactly about the girl that caught her attention.

Eva shrugs.

I'm not sure. Her face. Her gaze. Her cool demeanour.

Eva's wearing a thin black silk dress (a hand-me-down from me) and red Dr. Martens.

I logged on again yesterday, she says, and scrolled through all the faces until eventually I found her.

She finishes her coffee and pulls a face mask out of her pocket, stuffing it into the empty paper cup she then drops into the waste bin.

The girl's got pretty blue wallpaper on her wall, she says. Everyone can see each other's background, but it's impossible to make eye contact. Anyway, there are so many people logged on at the same time that she might be seeing entirely different faces from the ones I see. Maybe I'll signal and see if she reacts.

~

How do experiences live on, not as memories, but as absences? How to write about the splash of untranslatable white paint and make of it a story with a clear beginning, middle and end? When I was sixteen years old, between autumn 1982 and winter 1983, I knew for a brief time a forty-four-year-old man I'm calling K. He's old now. Sometimes I think about sending him an email.

*Remember me?*

He was always high or low or strung out on one thing or another, he was in demand and unpredictable.

It's unlikely that he remembers me. I don't know if I *want* him to.

I click on the photos of him on the Internet and I see an old man who's moved from New York to an entirely different setting (with a beach close by), who occasionally posts photos of himself, his children, his grandchildren and his thirty-years-younger wife on social media. The most recent are new, he's been uploading pictures while I've been writing about him, he doesn't know I'm thinking about him every day, repeating his name to myself. In one of the images, he's with his whole family, on a white-sand beach, around a big table that's been festively set, everyone's keeping a good distance from each other, it's windy, I can tell by the girls' hair and the flapping of the edges of the white tablecloth; the point of the picture, judging by everyone's expressions and gestures, is clearly to illustrate how difficult it is to share a birthday cake when everybody's wearing a face mask. The cake, with more than eighty candles on it, is the table's centrepiece. Untouched. Blue sea surrounds them. During the last few years, besides family photos, he's posted pictures from the seventies and eighties when he was most fêted, pictures of beautiful women, magazine covers, features, legendary fashion shoots, and it makes me wonder if he might ever post the picture he took of me. I know it won't happen. Of course it won't. If he remembers me, it certainly won't be as a career highlight, as someone who lit up his life. What was it he called me when I sat in his jeep and cried and said I wanted to go home, *a neurotic little bitch?*

All I have is a memory of a photograph of a young girl, of me. I was the same age then as Eva is today, even slightly younger, and I wonder if experiencing *sixteen* again, not as myself, but through another person, a child, a daughter, does something to one's perspective.

I'm no longer as furious as I used to be at the sixteen-year-old girl I once was, no longer as ashamed of her, as eager to write her off, forget her, pretend she didn't exist. *Doesn't* exist. And yet: the fact that no one remembers what happened, that it's never been written about, makes me wonder if what I experienced is true, whether it really happened, or rather I know it happened – *stupid little girl,*
  *why don't you go back home* – but I doubt whether what I experienced is valid, whether there's any point broaching it. And yet: if I don't write about it, because

I'm uncertain, because uncertainty creates anxiety, because I'll do almost anything to avoid anxiety, because uncertainty and anxiety transport me back to the same state of helplessness I knew at sixteen – then I'll fail to acknowledge, as Annie Ernaux writes, that *these things happened to me so that I might recount them.*

But the girl I was unravels whenever I draw near. There's so much you don't understand, she shouts from a street corner in what is to her an unfamiliar city. And the word *knew* is wrong, she says. You wrote, *When I was sixteen years old, between autumn 1982 and winter 1983, I knew for a brief time a forty-four-year-old man I'm calling K.*, that's wrong. It wasn't about knowing, getting to know.

    Be precise. Please.

It's the middle of the night, it's freezing out, she's wearing a borrowed dress, a new blue coat and knee-high boots.

~

In New York, K is surrounded by people. In the studio. In the apartment. There's the scrawny young assistant, the make-up artists and hair stylists, the friends, an older photographer who lives in an apartment in the same building. *He used to be famous, he took important pictures, you ought to know who he is*, K tells me. Girls. There are girls everywhere. And a fat man. The men (apart from the assistant) are old, over forty, over fifty. The fat man's name is Claude. Wherever K is, there's Claude. When K looks to the left, Claude looks to the left, when K looks to the right, Claude looks to the right. Apart from that, it's hard to know what exactly Claude does. He knows the names of all the girls who come and go. One of them is Jane. She goes to the same school as me, she's a freshman, I'm a junior, she's fourteen or fifteen, younger than me, but over six feet tall, talks to no one. When we run into each other at K's studio, we pretend not to know each other from school. As if our being in high school is a secret we prefer not to share. Jane was discovered in a shopping mall in Wisconsin. Rumour has it she's living with her agent.

Jane is incredibly pretty, I say to K.

Jane isn't pretty, Claude replies in his stead, she's a piece of sex.


Jane disappeared from school a few months after I came back from Paris. I look for her in the school yearbook for 1984, but can't find her anywhere.

What happened?

Someone said she quit modelling. Someone said she enrolled at another school. Someone said her agent kicked her out and replaced her with someone else. Someone said her older brother came and picked her up at Port Authority (he found her standing alone, towering above every other woman and almost every other man, underneath the Greyhound sign, without so much as a dollar in her pocket), someone said her brother wouldn't let go of her until they were safely back in Wisconsin, someone said the bus journey took almost nineteen hours, which is a long time not to let go, someone said she was dead, someone said she got a job in Milan, someone said she got a job in Tokyo, someone said she overdosed, crack, heroin, someone said she'd snorted so much coke she put a hole in her nose and couldn't work as a model any more, someone said she met a twenty-year-old guy, got married and moved away.

~

If I say your names many times, one after the other (all the names I've given you over the years), I can picture your face, your thin body, your hands (wings?) dry like old leaves, ivy in autumn.

When we were little, nine years old perhaps, and more sun than shade, warm, you took my hands in yours.
    Look at us, you said.
    I pulled my hands away.

It's bad luck to compare hands, I said, at least it is if you put them palm to palm.


You've started turning up unannounced, like when we were young.
 Leave me alone, I say. Go away and bother someone else.
 You lie down on the sofa. You take a seat in the chair by the window. You dance round and round in the sunshine, trembling, saying, *I'm not making any sound, I'm not making any sound, listen to how quiet I am.*
 And you take my hands in yours again and squeeze them tight.
 Your hands are bigger than mine, you say. Everything about you is bigger.

~

Spring 2021. I go to the old summer house to write.
 Mamma and I used to spend summers there when I was little. Mamma would play 'Raindrops Keep Fallin' on My Head' on the record player in the living room. She'd take pictures of everything (herself, me, the trees, the fjord, the cliffs) and pin them up on the wall after getting them developed in town. We'd walk barefoot over sun-warmed rocks, climb down the steep trail to the place where we'd swim, Mamma in long, airy

dresses and chunky cardigans that Eva, decades later, discovers in the closet and makes her own.


We'd eat stews for dinner that had simmered all day on the stove, and candy for dessert. I'd tell Mamma about the four weeks I spent with my father at Hammars (all of July), about his red bicycle, about my half-brother Daniel, who slept in the room next to mine, about the blue bed linen. In August, a week or two before the start of the school year, darkness fell quickly, and Heidi arrived by train. Mamma and I jumped up and down, waving on the platform. Heidi, who was a year older than me, could dive from the highest rocks and pick up lion's mane jellyfish with her bare hands.


Sometimes Mamma and Heidi would sit beside each other at the big table with the view of the fjord, the ocean and the lighthouse, and talk and laugh, sort the cutlery or play solitaire. They had long hair that shone in the dwindling sunlight.


On the small table, the one by the window, stood a blue bowl of overripe apples.

~

Don't take my pictures down, Mamma says on the phone.

For a long period, while no one can travel, she's been living in a house in Massachusetts.
   Things I know about my mother:
   She's fallen in love with a red maple outside her kitchen window.
   She lives with an old man who doesn't answer when she speaks to him.

~

If you're going to the summer house, I'm coming with you, you say. *You, you, you.* I don't know what to call you. I take the dog with me. He's as old as my mother's maple. Perhaps all I need to say is that he exists. *The dog exists.* Large, black-coated, beautiful. At night his breathing is so loud that I dream about trains (rattling, tooting) because he's lain down in bed next to me, sometimes on top of me, with his nose in my ear.

The first evening, I climb down the rocky trail to the fjord to look at the jellyfish. They're bobbing on the water's surface, fragile beings entangled in one another's tentacles, it's impossible to tell where one begins and another ends. Except for one, which is blue and not entangled in itself or bound up with the others. It's not as splendid as the one I dreamed about when I was little, but I stand looking at it for quite a while. It contracts and releases, contracts and releases. As I stand there looking – streams of late-spring sunlight on the water – I think of my heart, and my children's hearts, my invisible sister's (*your*) heart that doesn't exist, my father's heart that doesn't beat, my mother's heart.

What are you up to? Mamma asks on the phone.

I'm writing, I say, and translating bits and pieces in between. Right now, I'm working on a poem by Anne Sexton.

Are you there by yourself, then? she asks.

Yes, I say.

Have you taken my pictures down?

No, I say.

Do you ever get afraid of the dark?

Yes, I say, all the time.

What are you writing about?

Nothing important. This and that. Maybe something that'll make you laugh, like in Anne Sexton's poem, *that untamable, eternal, gut-driven ha-ha*, I was always able to make you laugh like that, remember?


In the morning and again in the evening – long walks with the dog on the country road past vivid green cornfields. The dog is trying to figure out what it means to be a dog. He's afraid of waves and barks at his own shadow, his ears are soft, his paws smell good. One day while we're out walking, he tugs and pulls on his lead, more so than usual, and to the astonishment of us both I begin to cry. The dog turns and looks at me forlornly, believing himself no doubt to be the cause of my tears. I shake my head. It's not your fault, I tell him, it's not your fault. *I can't explain.* Which is what I usually say when you – not the dog – appear.

I can't explain. You're different every time, appearing in ever new guises – as too bright a light, as a swarm of insects, as angry branches, as a polished black shoe. It's the shape-shifting that makes you impossible to be around. I might not recognize you, but I know it's you.

~

I do not have Mamma's permission. It's out of the question. You're much too young. *I'm saying no.* She spins round and round in the shadowy apartment on the Upper West Side saying no. How many ways can a person say it? Three, five, nine, eighteen, twenty-seven, fifty-nine, eighty-three, a hundred and five. And yet the girl on the plane is me. New blue coat, new knee-high boots, red woolly hat. *We travel dressed and ready* is what we say in our family, Mamma declares. I don't know if it's true. I've never heard anyone in our family say *we travel dressed and ready*, before or since.

Mamma said no, you're not going, you're too young, it's not appropriate, it's not okay, we don't know if these people are trustworthy. And then we went and bought new clothes for the trip.

When Mamma said *these people*, I believe she was referring to K, but it was easier to think and talk in general terms than to say anything specific, especially in matters affecting her, or me, or us.

~

The summer house is furnished with dressers of all sizes and of all kinds of wood. The drawers are stuffed full, one with forks, knives and spoons, another with photographs. I sort through the photographs. Mamma and her partner, her other half, are still young in them. They have friends visiting. They barbecue. They sit on the veranda. Everyone is drinking wine, except Mamma. She drinks Coca-Cola and sits in the shade beneath a big black sunhat. In a third drawer I find a folder containing things from the seventies and eighties: photos, magazine clippings, letters and a small wad of scribbled notes. One of them is a love letter. The handwriting is barely legible, but I make my way through it. The man writing (I think it's a man) quotes from Tove Jansson's *Moominland Midwinter*. Reading handwritten letters is a lost skill, like winding up a wristwatch, consulting an encyclopedia – or waiting to discover the answer to whatever it was you didn't know until you get to a place where there actually *is* an encyclopedia – or dialling a number on a rotary phone, preferably using a pencil if you're a girl and don't want to ruin your nails. I try to decipher the signature of whoever wrote the love letter, but eventually I give up.

I read the letter out loud to Mamma on the phone. I ask if she remembers who wrote it. It's either F or H, she says, probably F.

An old photograph of Mamma is pinned to the pine wall, hidden behind stacks of books. The picture is from the sixties, and reminiscent of the one K took of me some twenty years later. Both photographs depict a young, desirable woman with big blue eyes and bare shoulders.

The wad of scribbled notes is stuffed in an envelope. They're letters from me to Mamma. One is dated February 1983, a few weeks after I came home from Paris. All the notes are from about that time. The handwriting is almost identical to my handwriting today. An untidy, teetering hand. Mamma must have gathered the notes together in this envelope, taken them with her to Norway and then put them away in the drawer of the pine dresser here in the summer house with other items since forgotten.

> *Dear Mamma*
> *If you're sad about something — it's better you talk about it than get angry at me. I want you to trust me. Maybe that's hard. But I promise to tell you the truth if you want to ask me something. I know I've been horrible to you — and that you might not be able to forgive me yet. But I promise I'll never be like that again. All I want is for us to be friends (girlfriends). I love you very much.*

I picture her now, eighty-two years old, the phone pressed to her ear. I don't tell her about the note. *I know I've been horrible to you — and that you might not be able to forgive me yet.* I can't remember what it was that I'd done. Was it Paris? That I didn't stick to our agreement, that I broke my curfew, that I wasn't back at the hotel by 10 p.m.?

Mamma and I hang up. Though of course that's not what we do. We don't actually *hang up* even if it's what we say.
    *I'll hang up now. Do you want to hang up first?*

Her days, she says, are short and long at the same time. She goes from room to room, she prepares food, cleans, sets the table, leaves the TV on in the background, a constant stream of news. She talks to the cats, she washes her hair, exhaustion is like grief, and when I ask her how she's doing, she says in her usual way, *I don't want to go there now*, without specifying exactly where *there* is. She talks to her partner, her other half, who never answers when she asks him things, she says he's starting to forget things. She writes grocery lists, picks up the telephone, then puts it down, pulls the chair closer to the kitchen window and looks out at the red maple in the soft afternoon light.

~

On the plane I sit almost at the very back by the toilets, next to a man whose name is Claus – Claus with a C, he tells me, not the German spelling, like the war criminal Klaus. I'm not the Butcher of Lyon, he assures me. He was arrested in Bolivia, did you hear about it?

I nod. I saw it on the news this morning.

You must read the papers, he says, not watch television. A new plague is upon us, a terrible new disease, did you know?

I don't catch his surname. Claus something-or-other is a professor of literature and feeling quite ill. Or not ill, just out of sorts. I've got a cold one day, he says, then aching limbs the next. I'm running a temperature, though not that high, and my head feels too hot inside. Put your hand here, he says, indicating his brow. A fever, wouldn't you say? I demur with a shake of my head. We're still on the runway waiting to take off. When eventually the aircraft accelerates and angles into the sky, he breathes a sigh of relief and lights a cigarette. He smiles. Not much we can do now, he says, and gets his book out. No point tensing muscles and being attentive to every sound. If we crash, we crash. The book he is reading is Hermann Broch's *The Sleepwalkers, Part Three: The Realist, 1918*.

My father was born in 1918, I say, indicating the title.

Indeed, indeed, he says.

He's afraid of catching cold too, I add, and of fevers.

Aha, he says with a polite nod.

I get my own book out. It's dinner time. First peanuts and drinks. Claus and I lower our tables. He purchases a miniature of whisky and is handed a glass with ice cubes in it. I study the stewardess while she serves him his drink – tall, stringy, oldish, strict – and decide against ordering a gin and tonic for myself and ask for just plain tonic water instead. I'm always being asked for my ID, I look younger than nineteen, the age I *want* to look, and younger than sixteen, the age I *am*. After a while, the stewardess returns, this time with our meals. She takes two white plastic trays from her trolley and hands one to me and one to Claus. We eat (salty meat, gravy, a slice of white bread, a bite of cheese and a piece of cake wrapped in plastic) in silence. After the food, but before the lights are dimmed and the film starts, he asks if my feet are cold. He's noticed I'm sitting cross-legged in my seat with my feet tucked under me as if I were meditating, though he guesses I'm not the meditating type and that I'm in this position because my feet are cold.

Am I right?

A little bit, yes, I say.

He leans forward and opens his briefcase, which he'd pushed under the seat in front. He produces a pair of woolly socks, large, grey, home-knitted, and tells me he always keeps at least two pairs on long-haul flights, and on shorter ones too, for that matter. It's important to take what you might need in your hand luggage, he says. These are for you, for the duration, he says, and hands me the socks. Put them on, he says, your feet will soon be warm, you'll see.

And then he asks me what takes me to Paris.

I have work, I tell him as I pull the socks on, thinking about Mamma, who earlier in the day stood in the slush on the sidewalk to say goodbye, in a similar pair of soaking-wet woolly socks.

What about school?

I go to school, I tell him, but I have an assignment in Paris.

I don't say I'm a model, I don't look like a model.

What sort of work do you do? I ask, swiftly changing the subject from me to him.

I teach English literature, he says, though actually I don't have students any more, or classes, what I have is *office time* . . . I don't suppose you're in college yet?

I'm in high school, I say.

How old are you – fifteen, sixteen?

Sixteen. What do you do besides office time?

I'm writing a book.

About what?

A parable about the end of the world.

I see.

Do you?

Well, no.

Matthew twenty-five, one to thirteen.

I shake my head.

The parable of the ten virgins, he says.

I shake my head again and say maybe I heard about them in confirmation class. I can't remember . . . What was the story?

Five are wise and five are foolish, says Claus. That's the story. Five do okay and five don't. The wise ones do everything right, the foolish ones are . . . *unprepared*. And then the world ends. Did you know, I mean since we're talking about the number five, that the earthworm has five hearts?

I had no idea, I say.

I've got only one, he says, and points to his chest,

and I believe I've worn it out completely. They say the third heart attack is the one that kills you, but I can tell you I've had more than that.

Goodness.

Fifteen years old, he says, and mumbles to himself: *I hear the earthworm's song in the hearts of many girls.*

Sixteen, I say.

What?

Sixteen. You said fifteen. I'm sixteen.

Of course.

I drain what's left of my tonic water.

Is that why you've always got two pairs of woolly socks with you – so that you're prepared?

Yes, exactly, says Claus, exactly.

And while repeating the word *exactly*, as if he's not quite sure if it's the right word, the stewardess appears and pulls down the film screen. The cabin lights are dimmed. I look at my watch. It's still set to New York time. In five hours, we'll be landing in Paris.


Whenever I've started working on a new book, I've thought now is the time I'm going to write about the photograph K took of me in January 1983. I've long wanted to write about the time leading up to when it was taken, those days in Paris and the time after, but I've always ended up writing something else instead. The story about the photograph makes me sick, it's a shitty story. I've abandoned it a thousand and one different times for a thousand and one different reasons.

~

When I landed in Paris, Claude picked me up at the airport and drove me to the hotel where I was meant to stay. Claude, with his expensive watches proffered from a grubby overcoat. Claude, with his watery eyes. Claude, who drives too fast and hardly says a word.

~

When Mamma, in lockdown with her other half, calls from the house in Massachusetts and can't get hold of me, she leaves a message (often several, one after another) on my voicemail. Sometimes the connection is so bad that all I receive are fragments – as if the message were a two-thousand-year-old poem of which only the odd word has survived, and you have to imagine the rest. One night I dreamed that she lived in a small house surrounded by palm trees and vines. To get there you had to drive along a desolate road with swamp on either side and nobody in sight. Swamp and crocodiles. Often she finds herself (I imagine) on this exact road when she's calling me.

I listen to her messages as I walk past the vivid green cornfields.

] heart
] told the doctor that
] the bubbles and the light
]
]
] a proper answer after waiting days on end with
　　all that worry.

~

The dog and I climb down the hill. There's a long steep path down to the fjord. I'm not sure *path* is the right word. Or *trail*. Anything having to do with getting from one place to another — trails, paths, tracks — disconcerts me. I can lose my way, my bearings, my footing, at any moment, in any landscape, city or building. I clearly never grasped what Walter Benjamin refers to when writing about the art of getting lost: *Street names must speak to the urban wanderer like the snapping of dry twigs, and little streets in the heart of the city must reflect the times of day, for him, as clearly as a mountain valley.* There's no art to it, no pleasure, I'm suggesting a degree of getting lost where nothing speaks to you, not the street names, not the dry twigs, not the times of day. The first time I got lost like that was in

Paris. Everything was winter white, tinged with blue. This I remember clearly. It was the middle of the night. I was jet-lagged, Mamma was still awake but thousands of miles away, in another time zone, she'd called and called for hours without me picking up at the other end, I was sure of it, she'd spoken to the lady at the reception desk, the *manageress*, asking in faltering French if she'd seen the girl, her daughter, return since checking in that morning. The address of the hotel. The name. All these things I'd forgotten to write down. How stupid can you get? *Look after myself? All grown up?* I thought I knew what to look for, landmarks close to the hotel – a newsstand; a window display featuring rickety, half-dressed mannequins; a tree; a blinking traffic light – but I didn't know the order in which these things would have to appear for me to be sure I was heading in the right direction.

When I speak to my husband on the phone, we agree that when he and Eva and I come back to the house together this summer, we'll swim in the fjord every morning.

To get to the place where we swim: first a gentle descent down the smooth rock. Then a makeshift bridge, five planks knocked together, spanning a gully too wide to jump. Then a narrow and steep path with a rope railing

I sneered at when I was little but for which I'm grateful now. The view out to the fjord and ocean is dizzying. Which is another way of saying that here, on this trail, which isn't exactly a trail but just a slender path, I have to cling to the rope and keep my eyes on the rock in front of me. I don't dare look anywhere else – not at the waves, the boats, the sun or the cloudy horizon. Vertigo, I read somewhere, is as much a desire to fall as a fear of falling.

The dog and I emerge on to a flat area that provides a moment's respite, a little cluster of trees, only a few square metres, where heather, moss and bilberry mounds greet the eye in bursts of purple and green, and the twisted pines give the illusion of being part of something bigger than an insignificant perch, a copse pretending to be a forest. Then, a new, steep, wave-scoured rock, and here the dog wants to roll in a giant's kettle of black silt, but I tell him no, for in it lie the ghosts of all the dogs I've had before him. Finally, I climb down the old iron steps, bolted to the rock, descending into the water.

I swim. The dog will not. He lies on a ledge keeping watch.

Climbing back to the top, everything repeats, the cliffs, the path, the copse, the bridge, only now in reverse, and the trail, or path, doesn't seem quite so dizzying. I've wound my hair in a big blue towel and removed my sandals. The rock is warm against the soles of my feet.

~

There exists only a single surviving recording of Virginia Woolf, first broadcast by the BBC in 1937. Her voice is brighter than I'd imagined. Writing, she says, *is only a question of finding the right words and putting them in the right order.*

~

*Why did you come here? K asks.*
    *What do you mean?*
    *Instead of going to your hotel?*

~

I press the buzzer even though it's the middle of the night, open the entrance door and walk up all the stairs in the dark, first floor, second floor, third floor. A nightclub with two older girls, then trying to find my way back to my hotel, only I couldn't remember its name, or where it was, or the address, and I couldn't ask anyone but asked anyway, to no avail, because what was I supposed to ask?

The only thing I remembered was his address. Because I'd written it down on a piece of paper.

A man wearing a red scarf walked me all the way there.

~

I have a room at a one-star hotel, I'm on my way there now, maybe it's in the 5th arrondissement, *but where's that*, I don't know. The old couple with the huge white dog shake their heads and walk on. I don't remember what the hotel is called, or where it is. All this I can say in English, not in French, but if I come upon a person on the street that night who speaks English, there isn't much he or she can do to help. Where is your hotel? *I don't know.* What's the name of it? *I don't know.* Do you remember the address? *No.* The only thing I remember is *his* address. *So you have an address?*

Yes, or no, I don't know.

*4, rue des Anglais* – could that be K's address in Paris? I haven't given the address much thought until now, how important it is. I've been thinking about *him*. And the photograph he took of me. And the days we were together. But as I write this, I wonder whether I should make the address a part of the story, because what if, for once, I am remembering correctly and he really did live at 4, rue des Anglais – wouldn't that get closer to K's actual identity?

Someone he knew back then might say: Didn't you live there?

K might very well not remember me, but he's bound to remember where he lived in Paris, even if it was forty years ago.

And if he didn't live at 4, rue des Anglais, that would be amiss too. In that case, I'd be what they call an unreliable witness. Someone who can't be trusted.


I click on Google Earth and find rue des Anglais. I move the cursor up and down, back and forth. Number four has a red entrance door. I don't remember a red door. Maybe it's been painted. Maybe it wasn't number four. Maybe I dreamed it up. The way I once dreamed I had an English teacher called Mrs French (when I was twelve and wore braces and lived in a big yellow house with a garden two hours from New York by train).

I moved the cursor up and down the street one last time, as if expecting to see her there, a sixteen-year-old girl in a borrowed dress, a new coat, a red woolly hat and knee-high boots.

~

My hotel room – a big virginal four-poster bed in the middle – was two flights up in a run-down building *somewhere* in Paris. But where? I don't know. Be accurate. I can't. Be specific. I don't know how. Precision is the minimum requirement. Not just for writers and artists, but also for girls who claim they're old enough to travel across the Atlantic by themselves and have their picture taken. A grey-haired woman greeted me and checked me in, I think she was the manageress, or the owner, she looked over my shoulder to see if anyone was with me, *did she see Claude loitering on the pavement outside*, she handed me the key, a big, gilded key fastened to an even bigger medallion with the hotel's name engraved on it. She explained in French that I had to leave the key in reception whenever I left the premises, and that breakfast would be served between seven and eight thirty. I understood what she was saying if only because she kept pointing and gesticulating and ended every sentence as if she were asking a question. (I just wanted her to finish talking, instructing, questioning, and let me climb the stairs to my room. Claude was waiting for me on the pavement outside, maybe she knew him, maybe she was trying to stop me.) The questions she asked were: Do you understand what I'm saying, dear? Are you sure? You mustn't take the key with you when you go out, but leave it here at the reception desk, do you know why? Because it could go missing, and you appreciate the problems that would present, don't you? Breakfast is simple but good. You will be having breakfast, won't you, thin as you are?

She patted my cheek and shook her head on seeing how big and heavy my suitcase was. There were cats everywhere. They lay sleeping in the reception and on the carpeted stairs that led to the second floor. I bent down and stroked one that had curled into a ball outside my door. It stretched and purred, grey-blue with white paws.

~

A man tugs at my dress, which isn't even mine, I've borrowed it from one of the older girls, he's trying to rip it off, he wants to see me naked, he says, we're on the dance floor, in the middle of the dance floor. Another man gropes me and says (mumbles, breathes) that I'm wet. I shake my head. He says it again, only louder this time, we're seated around a table and he says it to everyone. She's wet. His buddy laughs. Wet and ready. He's wrong. I look at the others. I'm not . . . One of the older girls leans across the table and says in English, loud enough for everyone to hear, *Stupid little girl, if you can't handle people touching you, you shouldn't be here.* I feel a shudder pass through me, *I can handle it*, I mustn't cry, not in front of the others, I don't use tears to get what I want, I don't play-act. Inside, it's all flashing lights, music, loud voices, laughter. Sweat, heat. Outside – *I find my coat, my woolly hat, and get out* – it's night. It's snowing. I don't know where I am or where I'm going. I came here with the older girls. I thought I'd be leaving with them too. I walk down a street. And back up again. I'm lost. Or rather: being lost suggests you have an idea of where you were and where you are going, and that somewhere you took a wrong turn. I don't know where I am or where I'm going. The girls are still at the club. It's early evening in New York. If I'd had any money, I would have called home and talked to Mamma. If I'd had money and if there'd been a phone booth nearby. Mamma would be angry. The agreement was: If, against my will, you go to Paris by yourself, you're to be back in your hotel room by ten o'clock every evening. *I'll call you and say goodnight.* I check my wristwatch. It's 2 a.m. I try to picture my hotel, I try to picture it as hard as I can, as if by picturing it I could transport myself there. My suitcase is on the bed, a creaky four-poster affair fashioned out of dark wood, my clothes are strewn everywhere – on the bed, on the floor. I didn't change my clothes. Didn't shower. The bathroom was out in the hallway and occupied when I arrived. I tore the clothes out of my case, finding nothing to wear, what do you wear in Paris when you have no idea where you're going? I tried the belt around my coat, pulled my hat down over my ears.

How long have I been in Paris now? Seventeen hours. It's seventeen hours since I landed at the airport.

Again, I try to picture my hotel room. And then I picture my room at home in New York. I miss it. I walk down the street. Two young men go past on a moped. They shout something. I'm startled. I don't easily startle.

~

How long was I in my hotel room, how much time did it take to check in, tear all my clothes out of the case, not finding anything to wear? Probably no more than twenty minutes. Claude picked me up from the airport and drove me to the hotel. Hurry up, he said, quick, quick, quick, *vite, vite, vite*, his face all sweaty, his armpits too, even though it was January, and he was standing outside in the wintry chill in just his shirtsleeves, leaning against the car and waving me and my suitcase towards the hotel door. Quick, quick, he said, then we'll drive to the studio.

~

According to Michael L. Slepian there are thirty-eight different kinds of secrets. Slepian has spent over a decade researching secrecy and how it affects our lives. His research project developed gradually. In the beginning, he was interested in metaphors, which took him specifically to the metaphors of secrets: I'm *weighed down* by a secret. I'm *carrying* a secret. I'm *keeping* a secret. A secret, he suggests, isn't simply a matter of holding back in particular situations. Holding back is only a part of it. The secret exists and works within us even when we don't actively engage with it, in the sense of dodging a question, concealing what we know, diverting attention from it, or straight out lying. Secrecy, Slepian writes, begins with an intention, '. . . plenty of secrets don't require upkeep or lies to maintain,' he suggests. 'This is why we must define secrecy not as something we do, but as an intention: *I intend for people to not learn this thing.*' As soon as the intention to keep something secret arises, it starts working upon us as loneliness and melancholy.

*This is our secret.*
 *Yes.*
 *It's nobody's business what we do when we're alone together in this room.*
 *I know that.*
 *You're not to tell anyone.*
 *I won't tell anyone.*


If Slepian is right and secrets start as intentions, it makes me wonder when the secret between K and me started (in the elevator in New York, in his studio, in his Paris apartment) and how it then worked upon us. Has it been working upon him, even if I no longer exist to him? Not as a name, or as a photograph, or as a body, or as a face, or as a gaze, or as a taste, or as a smell, or as words, or as tears, *I want to go home, I want to go home, I don't want to be here any more.* If K can't remember me – the sixteen-year-old girl who turned up on his doorstep one night – is everything that happened between us (and which I promised not to tell anyone) still our secret? Or is it only mine?

~

Jet-lagged and disorientated that very first morning in Paris, in a red woolly hat and blue coat in the big studio without windows, like an illuminated bunker. K is photographing a girl in a long blue silk dress. Sleeveless. She does something with her long, thin arms, like a classical ballet dancer, a gracious, dismissive movement: *approach me not.* She's younger than me. K speaks to her in French. Later I find out she's not from Paris but from Montreal, that she's been flown in for several important assignments. Have I been *flown in* too? She's thirteen and staying with some older girls who are looking after her. I'm staying at a hotel. I don't remember the name. Claude sped me from the airport to the hotel, then from the hotel to the studio. There are lots of people at work. Make-up artists, hair stylists, editors, assistants. K's studio in Paris looks a lot like his studio in New York. Claude says hello to everyone, but first he goes straight up to K and hugs him. K hugs him in return. They slap each other's backs and exchange some words in French. Once, while we were still in New York, Claude hugged me. He didn't slap my back affably, but ran his hands over my breasts (or the sides of my breasts), my waist and my behind. Claude looks at the girl in the blue dress and smiles at her.

No one speaks to me. I'm still standing in the doorway, feet seesawing on the high threshold, partly hidden behind a big heavy door. I watch everyone, the way they know exactly how to move around the studio, and wonder where I should go.

Claude saunters over to the long table where breakfast has been laid out, and helps himself to croissants, coffee, fruit, jam. He lights a cigarette.

I hesitate, then cross the room, only to bump into a man with a comb in his hand who looks at me with exasperation, *watch where you're going*, I look down, carry on walking to where K is standing with his camera. He hasn't got much equipment. The lighting is simple. He doesn't want the girls too made-up. This is his trademark. *All natural.* When he isn't working as he is now, he carries a Leica. Snapping away.

I stand next to him.

He doesn't turn around.

Here I am, I say, adjusting my red hat.

My voice sounds strange, as if it hasn't been used in a long time.

K looks up from the camera. He laughs.

So I see, he says.

I landed a few hours ago. Claude picked me up from the airport.

Good.

I look around the studio.

Are you going to photograph me today?

No, I don't think so . . . Not today. Maybe tomorrow. We'll see.

Okay.

Why don't you find somewhere to sit.

Okay.


The girl in the blue dress is chewing gum, and in the few minutes K and I have been talking, she's assumed an expression that means to say she's bored to death. She can't fool me. The trick is to vacate your eyes. Split yourself in two. Become yourself and someone else at the same time. And then let that someone else — your invisible ghost sister — be the one doing the looking. Give her your gaze. Give her your fear, your awkwardness, your desire, your rage (which our mothers have told us to keep under wraps), your hope, your immaturity. Give it all to her, empty yourself entirely. When K picks up the camera again, the girl in the blue dress spits out her chewing gum into her hand hastily. She rolls it into a little ball between her thumb and index finger and sticks it to a Rubik's cube she's been playing with while

K has been talking to me. She puts the cube with the chewing gum on a high table in front of her stool. I notice she's almost solved it. She turns to K and gives him her full attention.

Beautiful, says K.

I walk over to the food table, realizing only now how hungry I am. And hot. The woolly hat itches. I take a little bit of everything that's on offer, piling food on to a plate. My stomach rumbles. I look around the big, busy space. Where am I supposed to go? Where can I sit? When I was little and you and I promised never to leave each other, I felt less alone when you were around, even though I knew you weren't real. Now it's different. I'm not *less* alone with you beside me, but *more*. Maybe because you combine not being real with a steady flow of directives and reprimands. *Take your coat off, keep it on, take your coat off, keep it on.* What am I meant to do? There's a leather sofa against a wall at the far end of the studio. I sit down on it after shoving several pieces of clothing to one side. A woman comes running towards me, yelling in French. She's waving and gesticulating. I don't understand what she's saying and wonder if maybe she wants me to hand her the clothes. I put my plate down carefully beside me on the sofa and lick strawberry jam from my fingers. *No, no, no,* she yells.

K turns to look. He rolls his eyes.

She wants you to sit somewhere else, he calls to me across the room. Because of the clothes, don't sit on the clothes. And don't get smudges on them.

I wasn't . . . I didn't.

But K has already turned away.

I get up with my plate and offer my apologies, *je suis désolée, je suis désolée*. How to say sorry is one of the few things I remember from French class. The woman rolls her eyes. First K, now the woman. Doesn't anyone in France know that after you've turned fourteen, rolling the eyes is completely unacceptable? I wonder if I'm going to eat all the food I've served myself – croissant, bread, melon, chocolate, jam, an overripe banana – and if so where I'm going to stand or sit without getting in the way, eat the food, *vite, vite, vite*, so I can get rid of the paper plate I'm holding, a thin white piece of cardboard, sagging and drooping unpredictably in my hand.

I can also just find a wastebasket and throw it away, take off my coat and woolly hat and conquer the room once and for all, but I'm too hungry, I can't do it, I have to find a place in a corner, somewhere I can eat.

~

It's five in the afternoon.
    I'm hungry again
   and
light-headed
and
sleepy.

*

I'm in Claude's car, this time in the back. K is in the passenger seat next to Claude.

They're speaking French.

Claude stops outside a building, *N° 4*, it says above the entrance.

K says goodbye to Claude and gets out.

Claude swivels to look at me, jerks his head indicating the door, as if saying *get out of the car*.

But aren't you taking me to my hotel?

Better if you get out here, Claude replies.

But I've got all my things at the hotel.

Here, he says, this is where you get out.

~

K opens the entrance door, I follow him up the stairs. He lives on the second floor. He doesn't turn around to see if I'm there, he knows it. He apologizes for the dark staircase. Usually the lights go on and off by themselves, he says, but there's something wrong with the wiring, things haven't been working for a few days. Inside the apartment he turns on the lights, rolls a joint, gestures a *make yourself at home*, or a *sit down*, or a *this is where I live*. I take off the blue coat, fold it and put it on the round table. I put my red woolly hat on top, then smooth the little pile as if it were fresh linen taken down from a clothes line. I sit down on a straight-back chair by the window. We spend a few hours there, after which we go to a dinner, then at half past two in the morning I return to the apartment. But I don't know any of this then.

I wonder now, as I'm writing this, if K knew. If he knew all along that the girl would come back. I wonder now if K had planned to make a play for the girl ever since he saw her in the elevator in New York in the autumn of 1982. I wonder about these things, because the fifty-five-year-old writer I am today knows a lot more about planning and thinking through the consequences – *if I do this, she'll do that* – than the sixteen-year-old girl did.

K paces the room. He smokes. He can't sit still while smoking. I don't know why. I ask if he can take me to my hotel. I hear our voices far away. He shakes his head. *No.* We're going to dinner soon. You're coming with me. Important people will be there. It'll be good for you to be seen. So when you're introduced to Z – make sure he sees you, okay?

Yes, but I'm hungry now. I try not to cry.

He halts abruptly, tokes his joint. He looks at me. Can you please stop? *Hungry thirsty take me here take me there.* Want some? He hands me the joint; how many has he rolled? I've lost count. Maybe it'll relax you. I shake my head. A drink, then? He fetches two glasses and a bottle of gin. Yes, please. He opens the bottle, pours two shots, puts the bottle down on the table. He crouches calmly in front of me. He wraps his arms around my legs and puts his head in my lap.

You're so beautiful, he says, with almost no

make-up on. *I'm glad you're here.* He looks up and his eyes find mine. *Really.* We're going to do great work together, he says. First tomorrow – he says tomorrow's client's name – and then, later in the week, French *Vogue* no less. If everything works out, you understand. I nod, still light-headed. Gin on an empty stomach. Jet-lagged. I look at the time, it's only midday in New York, where Mamma is. I wonder if I'm going to be sick and what K will say if I throw up in front of him.

But do you think you could run me by my hotel on the way to dinner?

K gets to his feet and starts pacing again.

I need for you not to act like a child now, he says.

But do you know the name of the hotel?

For crying out loud, no, I've no idea.

He goes over to the bookshelf, opens first one book, then another, then tears out a page.

Here, he says, and places the torn-out page on the table in front of me. He finds a pen in his jacket pocket and puts it on the table too.

Here, he says again, write down my address and phone number in case we get separated. Okay?

Okay.

~

In spring 2016, my English translator and I were reviewing the text of one of my novels when during the course of that work I sank into a depression that was different, more alienating, and felt more perilous than previous depressions. It passed after a few months, and I found myself once again getting up early in the morning, having breakfast, walking the dog, spending time with my family. But then, in autumn 2019, it came back, the same strange ghost, maybe it was you. Because it was around then, when the new depression came back, that you appeared under an elm tree in the park. I didn't want to die, but death was woven into everything. *Nothing is ordinary any more*, you said. Everything is prickly sunlight and unrelenting darkness. God doesn't exist. People don't exist. The world doesn't exist.

Your children and your husband exist, of course, but on the other side of an invisible wall, cold to the touch, a wall only you can see and against which you hurl yourself again and again.

Your children, your dog, your family, the mealtimes, early mornings, late afternoons, *what happened today*, *oh yes*, *let me tell you*, the children's homework, the late-night snacks, the switching on and off of lights. All that. Behind the wall. The fear makes you distant and unapproachable, afraid of everything.

You cry a lot, like clockwork, half past eight in the morning, four in the afternoon, ten at night. And then the times change. Just when you thought you had identified a pattern, there's a new schedule for despair.

It was the same when you were pregnant – the nausea and light-headedness would come at appointed hours that went on to change.

I sit down at my desk, every day, and try to translate a few pieces, poems mainly, like the one about melancholy by Jane Kenyon, pieces by others, especially women, women who write, who wrote, who were here on earth before me. This time the depression won't go away.

*I'll never leave you.*

But sometimes there's a blessed pause – like a sudden breath of cool wind from an open window like when you and I were little and lay in bed with a fever and then our mother would come in and shake the duvet and air the room. And yet every time I think, *But it's getting better now*, Eva's voice in the other room, the dog's breath against my cheek, you come rushing as if you smell blood.

~

Some people said it was a mistake to call my last book a novel when it was based on real events. I don't know. When I was writing it, I thought mostly about the order of events, the ones I remembered and the ones I'd forgotten and which I had to imagine. Here too I'm trying to create order.

*

When I was little I called you Ylva-li, like the girl in the story by Astrid Lindgren. Do you remember the rose bush, the underworld, the lake, the horses and the forest?

Eventually the English translation of my novel was finished, my translator and I agreed we were done, but I didn't start writing this new book, even though I lied and told everyone I was hard at work on it.

You appeared under the elm tree and insisted on walking beside me. You used to be called Ylva-li. I don't know what you're called now.

~

A few years ago, a journalist texted me: *Hi ☺ I'd like to talk to you about what's real and what's made up in your latest book. Have you got three minutes for a chat?*

The wording of the question distracted me and I got to thinking about the three minutes. What was I supposed to answer? It takes more than three minutes to count all the trees in Torshovparken and less than three minutes to walk around the bronze doll's head in Torshovdalen, but it takes three minutes exactly (if you don't walk too quickly or too slowly) to walk from one park to the other, from Torshovparken to Torshovdalen, from the park to the valley. The bronze doll's head is seven metres tall and modelled on one the artist,

Marianne Heske, bought at a flea market in Paris in 1971, twelve years before I went there to be photographed. It took three minutes (more or less) for me to take off my clothes and lie down beside K and feel his cock swell against my bare thigh and then to understand, with my whole being, that I couldn't just get up from the bed again, put my clothes back on and leave. Not now, too much time had passed.

You sit on the windowsill and are real and imaginary at the same time. You ask for a body. You ask for a mouth. You ask for memories. You ask me to be precise.

Autumn 2019. You turned up in September. What's the expression? *Out of the blue*. It wasn't just the new book I was out of sorts with, the one I said I was writing, but wasn't. All this lying about writing. I had no idea when I started out that there'd been so much of it. That autumn I bled a lot, and irregularly, as I did when I was a young girl. (After the days with K in Paris I stopped bleeding completely for more than a year.) At night I tore off one damp top after another. The temperatures were out of whack. Either it was too hot or too cold, or both at once. I didn't recognize my body. Or my brain. The word *composure* is defined as *the state of being calm and in control of your feelings or behaviour*. I was afraid I was losing all that. That is to say: losing my composure.

One season followed another. Winter 2019, winter 2020. The ice is melting. Eva sent me a text: *Loss of ice results in the suffering and death of polar bears, walruses, reindeer, arctic foxes and snowy owls.*

~

The girl runs through me.

But where was I supposed to go? I went to him because I couldn't find my hotel. I couldn't remember what it was called or where it was. The only address I remember, because I wrote it down, is K's.

~

The girl I used to be turns and looks at me. Her eyes are blue. She stands alone on a street corner with a piece of paper in her hand. Written on the piece of paper is an address. I can either keep on walking up and down, looking for a hotel I don't know the name of, or I can ask the next person I meet (a man, it turns out, who offers to walk with me) if they can help me find the one address I have. *Written down.* She waves the piece of paper in the air.

*Tell me what I'm supposed to do?*

Mamma has been calling and calling. She's woken up the manageress, who has struggled up all the stairs and knocked on my door.

*I'm sorry, Madame, she is not here. I have not seen her since this morning when she checked in.*

In writing down what happened, by telling the story as truthfully as I can, I'm trying to bring them together in one body — the woman from 2021 and the girl from 1983. I don't know if it can be done.

~

I go into the bathroom. I splash hot water on my face. I sit down on the bathroom floor, also blue. Not like the coat, not like the jellyfish, but like the blue in Mamma's blue-and-white porcelain tea set. I rest my head between my knees. The coat prickles. Such a warm coat isn't meant to be worn indoors, at least not for any length of time. This is exactly what the sales assistant at Bloomingdale's said a few weeks before. *You put it on, see if it fits, take it off.* I'd kept mine on and gone from mirror to mirror in the Women's Coats and Jackets department until I was so hot, I fainted. Or nearly fainted. I'm falling, I said. When I emerge from the bathroom, K is naked in bed. I undress too, he doesn't tell me to, but I understand it's what I'm supposed to do, first the coat, then the rest, feeling the cold air from the open window and the warmth of his body as I lie down beside him under the duvet. The bed is a mattress on the floor. The linen is white. There are no curtains in front of the windows, outside it's started to snow. His skin is old, like tanned hide. I'm not a virgin, but I've never felt skin like this before.

II

Red

*I had a terror since September,* Emily Dickinson writes in a letter, spring 1862, *I could tell to none; and so I sing, as the boy does by the burying ground, because I am afraid.*

I couldn't tell anyone, so I sing, because I am afraid. I can't write, I can't even translate the word *terror* — I can't find a word in Norwegian to accord with what Emily Dickinson meant back then.

*Why not?*

You're sitting on my shoulder in the guise of a red bird, pecking at my ear.

Because no matter what word I choose in Norwegian, it will mean something different from what I want it to mean.

Peck, peck, peck.

You too came in September. *You, you, you.*

It was then, in autumn 2019, that you appeared under the elm tree. At first you were just a dazzling light. I was struggling to write – to write the new book I kept saying I was writing but wasn't, to write anything at all, text messages, grocery lists, struggling with an existence that had been reduced (or perhaps oxidized) into a chaos of half-truths and approximations. Friendships were lost, I stopped answering letters, emails, texts. It felt as if the people I was closest to had stopped speaking truthfully about important matters – or what I thought were important matters. I didn't think about it then, but not speaking truthfully about important matters was becoming a strain, discordant, all-consuming.

Telling no one, I went back to bed every morning, after my husband had left for work and Eva had gone to school. Sleep was more biddable during the day than at night. I shook the duvets and smoothed the sheets, tidied the bedside table, opened the window wide and flung the curtains apart. I wanted air and light to stream to where I lay in the white linen – and sounds that told of a city that was awake.

But then sleep vanished. Night after night I kept my husband up for hours, until sleep took him, but not me. I'd get up and lie on the sofa instead. When the trembling started, the dog would come and lie down beside me (though there wasn't nearly enough room for the two of us) or at the foot end. His breathing was so loud. His grizzled snout kept going – warm, insistent, beautifully constant – like a machine pounding away in a factory all night long. In and out. In and out. I'd sung for my children when they were little. I'd sung for my father when he lay dying. I tried, quietly, in time to the dog's breathing, to sing now too, but you can't sing yourself to sleep.

For far too long the cutlery had been lying hotchpotch in the top drawer in the kitchen. I didn't like it. There was something careless about it. Not just the cutlery, but everything. I tidied the drawer. Now there was order of a sort. Forks lay with forks, knives with knives, spoons with spoons. I liked the spoons the best. I liked their big oval heads.

I talked to strangers – too long, too fast and too loud, and spent money I didn't have. I don't think anyone noticed. Or if they did, they never mentioned it to me.

When I type K's name next to my own in the search bar, I get no hits.

And I lost weight. I wondered if I'd be dead before the book was written or even properly started. *Maybe you shouldn't be writing at all now that you're ill* said the analyst, the first of many, a woman in her fifties. I thought about all the locked-up, deranged, depressed and frightened women throughout history who've been prescribed a course of treatment consisting of do-not-speak, do-not-write, do-not-say-a-word-about-the-rage-and-despair.

Janet Frame: *'For your own good' is a persuasive argument that will eventually make man agree to his own destruction.*

It was September 2019 and the Bahamas were hit by Hurricane Dorian. Seventy-three people lost their lives. Only a few days after tens of pine-nut harvesters were killed by a drone in Afghanistan's Nangarhar province and some forty wedding guests perished in Helmand in a raid supported by American air attacks. Young people went on strike for the environment. Eva was one of them. She sent me a clip of the one-minute-long roar outside Parliament.

I sit at the white kitchen table with a view of the park looking at old photos of a fourteen-year-old girl wearing a festive *bunad*. She's standing beside her mother, she too *bunad*-clad. The photos show mother and daughter surrounded by relatives who have travelled to New York from Norway and Canada to celebrate. The girl is pale. A sadness I haven't noticed before has fallen across her face.

A year and a half before I meet K in the elevator, I'm confirmed in the Norwegian Seamen's Church in Brooklyn.

It's Sunday, 24 May 1981. I know the girl in the photographs, the girl whose name is the same as mine, and who on the day of her confirmation has heard the congregation ask God to strengthen and bless her, the same girl who drank herself into a stupor the night before. I know she remembers nothing about that night. I know that at the time she's fascinated by, rather than concerned about, great swathes of time disappearing from her mind. I know that she hopes her mother won't notice that her breath reeks of alcohol and vomit despite all the toothpaste, mouthwash and chewing gum she's used. Her hair reeks too, her fingertips, her armpits. It doesn't matter how much she washes, the smell won't go away.

They must have sat down to lunch right after the photos were taken, there, in the shadowy apartment on the thirteenth floor. The mother had written a celebratory song, had it typed up and photocopied, so that all the guests could sing it together. Ham and vegetables in aspic were served. The girl didn't eat. The tune was that of a Norwegian lullaby and one of the verses ran like this:

> *Now is the change you've been waiting for*
> *From this day on you're a child no more*
> *Start out into life*
> *Its joys and strife*
> *Throw open the door!*

Two young people were confirmed that day in May at the Norwegian Seamen's Church in Brooklyn: the girl and a boy. He looked scared. I remember that. Like a freaked-out little kid. I obviously thought of myself as a lot older and savvier. Our preparation consisted of a thirty-minute lesson in the pastor's office every other week after Sunday service. The pastor seemed to have forgotten all about us, his two confirmands, every time we presented ourselves. It has occurred to me in retrospect that I never said anything to him about his sermons. I probably should have. Perhaps he thought I didn't care, which I did, I just didn't know what to say to him, often I'd been too hungover to say anything at all.

Every other Sunday I was taken to church by a specially hired driver. His instructions were brief: drive the girl to Brooklyn, wait for her outside the church, take her back to Manhattan.

It was the same driver every time. Thin, fair-haired, small hands. He said I could ride shotgun if I wanted. He said he liked my tulip miniskirt, he said I looked like Twiggy. Did I know who that was? I went to the school library the following Monday and asked the librarian if she could help me find pictures of Twiggy. Not the way she looked in 1981, but in the sixties when she was young. The librarian, a woman in her forties, got up from behind her desk and asked me to follow her. The reason she was given the name Twiggy, she said, was because she was so skinny. Get it? A stack of old magazines and a couple of books were retrieved from the shelves. Like a twig, just like you.

The drive from the Upper West Side in Manhattan to 33 First Place in Brooklyn took half an hour. Almost immediately, the driver got into the habit of stroking the inside of my thighs. He'd drive with one hand and stroke with the other. I stared straight ahead, didn't do anything to stop him, but tried not to look at his hand and what it was doing, what part of me it was touching. It was such a slender hand, like that of a child. After a few trips we stopped talking altogether, though he continued the stroking. He said nothing more about me looking like Twiggy, not even when I had my hair cut like hers. Confirmation classes started in January and the cherry trees in Central Park now blossomed. After many drives back and forth in silence, always the same, he finally opened his mouth and said something. It was April or early May, we didn't have many journeys left. He said that the next time he picked me up he hoped I'd have got rid of my black tights. It's better without them, he said.

He went quiet again, as if searching his brain for further words of clarification. And then, finally: It's springtime, he said, no tights neccessary!

The pastor reminded us that it was called *confirmation preparation* for a reason. He asked us if we'd ever thought about why it was referred to as *preparation*. What did it mean to be ready for something? The boy looked down. I shook my head. The pastor picked the black Bible up from his desk and read out loud: *And they that were ready went in with him to the marriage: and the door was shut. Afterwards came also the other virgins* – the *foolish* virgins, the *silly* virgins – *saying, Lord, Lord, open to us. But he answered and said, Verily I say unto you, I know you not.*


The fourth verse in Mamma's confirmation song concluded with the following instruction:

> *Allow me to give you this advice:*
> *Laugh at yourself without thinking twice!*
> *Give joy a stage*
> *Forget your rage*
> *And always be nice.*


What lingers in the body, like remnants of memories, are the headaches and a rumbling of the belly, as if I'm constantly starving but without any appetite. Sunday, 24 May 1981 is warm and sunny in New York (I've googled the weather for that day), almost twenty-five degrees Celsius. The *bunad* is a cumbersome affair, like some peculiar theatre costume rather than a festive dress, and much too woolly under the blistering sun. The last series of family photographs were taken outside on the sidewalk, under the green canopy. She is fourteen years old and hungover. Perhaps it's the alcohol that makes her face appear sad. Perhaps it's something else. I don't know. Part of the problem I have in writing this book is the idea of causality. For example: that the reason the girl looks cheerless on the day of her confirmation is that she was drunk the night before, or that she never said a word all those times driving back and forth to Brooklyn. *Forget your rage.* That the reason she had a terror in the autumn of 2019 is due to a series of events that took place in the spring of 1981 in New York, or the winter of 1983 in Paris, or long before that, or much later. Is that it? Will fear release its grip if I discover its origins? Will you pale and leave me alone? Is that what I want – for you to disappear? Cautiously I draw a line between the girl I was and the woman I became, and the only thing they have in common is a splash of white paint where the face should be. The stiff blouse of the *bunad* is soaked with sweat. The brooch hasn't been properly fastened to the collar.

Every time it comes undone, she feels the needle pricking at her throat.

The part of her body where the brooch-pin pricked. The poet Alice Oswald writes about it in *Memorial*, her book-length poem that's also a lament for the dead warriors in the *Iliad*:

> *But a spear found out the little patch of white*
> *Between his collarbone and his throat*
> *Just exactly where a man's soul sits . . .*

An analyst I'll refer to as Irene looks up from her notes and says she doesn't think my problem is depression – it's not depression, it's not anxiety.

So what is it?

It's about rage, she says. You're very angry, but you conceal it. You keep your feelings to yourself.

But that's not true, I say, I show my feelings and get angry all the time. Really. It's a problem. I lose my temper and say things I shouldn't.

Yes, but I don't mean *that* anger, Irene says impatiently, flipping through her notes, I mean the other anger.

The other anger?

Exactly.
What other anger?
The one you're unable to express, she says.


Other parts of the body that are soft and unprotected: the eyes. The belly. A small patch of skin directly under my breast.

Some years ago I saw a nature programme on TV. The camera zoomed in on some strange marks that looked like they'd been etched into a rock face, red flecks that perhaps could have been handprints. They turned out to be traces of a prehistoric bird. I have a cluster of small burn marks under my breast that look exactly like those marks in the rock. They stem from a very long day in the sun when I was fifteen. The marks, flecks, traces, imprints, come and go, sometimes they'll be gone for years, only to reappear, as if to remind me that it's my skin, my breast, and that the body will not forget even if I do.

The dog and I walked down Vogts Street, our movements even more out of sync than the day before. Now and again the dog turned his head and looked at me. I couldn't hide from him that something was off. My gait. My wobble. My legs turning into dandelion stalks. One step, two steps, three steps – heart beating. The heart knows before the brain that something's amiss.

Please stop pulling and tugging your lead, I said to the dog, as gently as I could, but my voice sounded strange, distant.

We both knew, the dog and I, that he wasn't the problem.

And then I stumbled. I don't know if *stumble* is the right word, because stumbling generally leads to a fall, which wasn't what I did. I didn't fall. I ascended into the air. It *felt* like I stumbled. It *felt* like I fell. Only I didn't end up flat on the pavement, dismayed and embarrassed, as fellow humans, other pedestrians, came hurrying to see what had happened. If only I had fallen. Injured myself. Landed on my face like an idiot and lain there bravely smiling. I lost my balance, that's true, but then instead of falling I ascended into the air. Not much, but enough for my feet to no longer touch the ground. And the funny thing was, I couldn't come down again.

I tugged on the lead, trying to *haul* myself down, tugged and tugged, until the dog began whimpering and licking my hand.

I'm sorry, I cried, I'm sorry.

I wanted to bend down and pat him, feel his thick black coat against the palms of my hands, bury my face into his neck, but I didn't dare move.

All that tugging on the lead had just made things worse, not just for the dog, who could barely breathe, but for me too, because now I ascended even higher. Hovering – soaring – ten centimetres, twenty centimetres off the ground. I don't know how high exactly. I've never been much good with either measurements or directions.

The dog licked my hand.

*Thank you*, I said and was startled by the sound of my voice, thank you for your big wet nose, for your lovely paws, for being such a good dog, a *real* dog, and then I said, quietly, so only he could hear me, I think we have to wait a while, until this thing passes.


Perhaps it had to do with lack of sleep. Or having lost all that weight. I don't know how long I stood (hovered, soared) there on the corner of Vogts Street and Torshov

Street. Or how many times it's happened since. I don't know how to make it stop when it starts.

*Scared, scared, scared, scared, scared.*

Across the street there was a new doctor's surgery with large tinted windows. *Disturbing.* My brain seemed unable, at least there and then, to absorb the fact that I was levitating and couldn't come back down, so it turned to other things instead: the tinted windows of the doctor's surgery and the suffering that probably went on behind them; what I would make for dinner if I ever got home again; whether Eva had remembered to take her maths book with her to school that day – and yes, Eva, my darling, I should have turned around and looked at her that morning when she was trying to tell me something, I should have listened to her.


Don't move, you said.

*You, you, you.*

I don't want you here! Go away!

Don't breathe, you replied.

I'm not breathing.

If you try to go any further, if you try to take even a single step forward, you said with a disinterested yawn, if you move your body even just a little bit, you'll just keep rising.


So yes. I did as you said. I didn't move.

How long do I have to stay like this?

For ever, you replied. It will never pass.

The dog, that beloved dog, sat down on the pavement and waited patiently.

Why couldn't you have come back to help me, why did you have to come back as this?


As what?


As an absence of vitality . . . as a diagnosis.

The dog and I soar (bob, glide, float) through Torshovparken, the trees shed their leaves, the leaves flutter to the ground, red and brown and orange, and after a time they collect in piles; I avoid the half-written (or more exactly: the yet-to-be-started) book about the girl from 1983.


Why do you call it a novel when everyone knows it's you?
    You've been following me around for a while and now you insist on our walking together. Everyone *doesn't know* it's me, I say, a little too loud.
    Is that me walking among the park trees, talking to myself and gesticulating?
    *Don't do that!*
    She who refers to herself in the first person is me and not me. The same as you, I say as gently as I can.
    You ask a hundred thousand questions and never wait for an answer before you ask the next one, you always want more, you never shut up.


One evening a few days before the incident in Vogts Street I stand naked in front of my husband.

I'm so skinny now – look at me! – I'm so skinny now that the doctor says I have to call her if I lose any more weight. Do you think I'm skinny, I mean *too* skinny, sick-skinny, my jeans don't fit any more, they're so loose, can't you see?

No, he says.

No, I say, what do you mean, no?

He takes a breath and looks away.

A little bit skinnier, yes, but not alarmingly so.


The USA has now formally withdrawn from the Paris Agreement, Eva informs me in a text. Fires rage in Australia, there are riots in Hong Kong.

You've placed yourself comfortably in my bones.

For five and a half hours, you would have been able – if you were really real – to see Mercury pass in front of the sun, a small black dot.

I was referred to a psychiatrist, a Dr Hegg.


Dear Hegg, I'll try to express myself clearly. I know you have no patience with whiners. I need help. My brain reminds me of a sentence in an Anne Sexton poem: *Ugly angels spoke to me.* I know you don't know who Anne Sexton is, and that you don't care. She wrote . . . what I'm trying to say is that I've started translating things from English into Norwegian. Not because anyone asked me to, but because it helps to look for the precise word. Passages from novels . . . poems . . . Mostly women, women who write, I mean, women who were here before me and who've been where I am now. Many of them dead. Some still living. What I'm trying to say is that I think of these women, the living and the dead, as benevolent ghosts, do you see what I mean? They spent their lives looking for the right words and putting them in the right order. And by doing that over and over again, they tell us we're not alone. Do you feel alone? I translate from English to Norwegian to ease the dread, that's what I'm trying to say, only I'm worried that all my blood is pouring out of me, that I'm losing a lot of weight. I may be running a temperature. And there's something else too that's hard to explain. My feet — I can't stand or walk. The ground keeps disappearing from under me. I daren't go outside, and my dog's not getting his daily walks. I'm scared.

Hegg smiled, he did so often, albeit coldly. As if the point of the smile wasn't to smile, but to show me all his teeth.

I sat on his sofa weeping and feeling ashamed of myself for weeping. Hegg wanted to give me one pill for sleep, two for depression, three for anxiety, or maybe it was a different way round, one for anxiety, two for sleep and three for depression. He said it was obvious I was ill. I told him I was hovering (soaring, bobbing, floating) and asked if he could see. He said he couldn't say one way or the other. But the only thing I wanted was for him to say I *wasn't* soaring. That he could *see* I wasn't. I won't be medicated, I told him. I want to get through this without pills. I've been like this before — like what? — afraid all the time, but then it goes away. The dread, I mean. He shook his head. You're not well, he said. His teeth rattling. He's made it his speciality to *call a spade a spade*, to never humour his clients. What do you suggest then, he said, if you don't want medication? I think I said I needed solace, to which he replied that solace wasn't his job.

And now his patience had run out. He looked at his watch. I had booked a double session, something he now surely regretted having agreed to.

Most of what I wanted to say, for instance that you had come back, I kept to myself. I said nothing about the red bird, its pecking beak. I said nothing about trembling all night, as if in the convulsions of laughter or a dance.

The dog wants me to take him for walks. I pretend not to understand what he wants when he appears in the bedroom in the middle of the day and puts his paw on the edge of the bed.

Do you remember what calm is, the dog asks, do you remember how calm feels, its ballast in the body, can you please try to remember that so we can go for our walks again soon?

When I was a child, I practised swimming in the ocean. I practised holding my breath. I practised twirling round and round until I got so dizzy I fell down. In the evenings, Mamma read aloud to me. Sometimes she sang too, though it never sounded very pretty. It didn't matter. I wasn't listening. It was the murmur I'd hear, not the song. I'd lie with my head resting on her tummy, having moved the sweater or blouse or dress or whatever she was wearing. Shall I sing another song? she'd sing, and then she'd sing another, and another, my cheek against her tummy. Her skin tasted of salt. It was like lying with a great pink seashell to my ear.

And another time, before that –

Mamma and I are walking up a long hill. She in front, me behind. How old are we? I'm five perhaps, and she's thirty-two. We've been to the post office and collected a parcel that's addressed to me. We don't know who it's from.

*

Who sent the parcel?

I don't know.

Can we open it right away? No.

Why not?

Because you don't just open a parcel as soon as you've collected it from the post office, you have to wait until you get home.

Why?

On most days Mamma gathers her long hair in a high ponytail. She looks like a girl then. Older than me, but still a girl.

Because patience is a virtue.


A few months earlier I received a letter from one of Mamma's suitors, an American. I can no longer remember what the letter said, or why this particular suitor wrote me a letter, but I do remember that he enclosed a photo. Perhaps he wanted me to remind Mamma of his existence. The photo shows him standing underneath a palm tree, smiling at the camera. He's sharply dressed in brown flared slacks, a brown wide-collared silk shirt and dark aviator sunglasses.


I wasn't the only one who loved my mother, and this was something I had to take into consideration every time I thought deeply about things.

*

I stuck the American's photo on the flowery wallpaper in my room, on top of one of the poppies. A framed photograph of my father already hung on the wall, but it was the American's face I looked at before falling asleep at night, perhaps because of his smile and because he'd written the words *I love you* on the picture. My father, in his green woollen turtleneck, gazed at me with a solemn expression, his lips firmly sealed. It was a very long time since I'd last seen him. I scarcely thought about him.

Mamma and I are walking up the long hill to the house.
    Mamma leads the way with grocery bags in both hands, I follow on behind, holding the parcel in front of me like a king's crown.
    What do you think it is?
    I don't know.
    But what do you think?
    I don't know.
    Who do you think it's from?
    Well, we'll have to find out when we get home.

It's summer. Mamma protects herself from the sun by wearing her long, airy, gooseberry-red dress and a big black sun hat. This is why – because of the big hat – her hair isn't in a ponytail when we're out walking.

\*

Mamma starts to sing, or hum, *one two, one two, one shovel and one shoe.* After a moment, I join in, *one two, one two, one shovel and one shoe.* Mamma's strong back, Mamma's long, strong legs, partly visible through the flimsy material of her dress, Mamma's sun-nipped ankles.

Up the hill we go. It takes time. Things take time. Patience is a virtue. But when I'm a grown-up and someone sends me a parcel in the post, I'm going to open it right away. No one's going to tell me I have to wait.

Around this same time, the summer of 1971, the Soviet space capsule *Soyuz 11* lands in the desert of Kazakhstan. Now and then, before bedtime, Mamma tells me about space – the moon, the stars, the abandoned dog. The cosmonauts were discovered to be dead after twenty-four days in orbit. Perhaps it was the state of weightlessness that killed them? A lot of people argued that this was indeed the case. Richard Nixon sent a letter of condolence. Many people (Mamma among them) asked themselves: How long can we live in weightlessness?

We've walked all the way up the hill now. Mamma stops, puts the grocery bags down, removes her sun hat and pulls her hair away from her face. Eleven and a half years later, in January 1983, she performs exactly the same gesture. It strikes me as I'm writing this that such movements, these fleeting moments in time – Mamma removing her sun hat, for example, and then pulling her hair away from her face – never presented themselves as meaningful when they occurred. It's strange that I should remember them, especially in view of everything I've forgotten. Forgetfulness is greater than memory. You may ask me: What happened between then and then? *I don't know*. How did you get from there to there? *I don't know*. All I have are movements – tiny, transient, insignificant gestures – that have attached themselves to memory and which connect the girl of 1971 to the girl of 1983 to the woman of 2021. I'm sixteen years old and about to get into the yellow cab that will take me to the Air France terminal at JFK. Mamma removes, not her sun hat this time, but her red woolly hat, and pulls her hair away from her face.

This is what I remember: She – Mamma – was standing outside the building with the green canopy. She'd taken the elevator thirteen floors down and run out on to the sidewalk without her shoes. Her long hair was blowing all over the place. She'd said no. No question about it. You're not going. She's weak at the knees and nauseous. Weightless. A snowstorm had been forecast, but it never came. I guess she was hoping it would snow so much the airports would be forced to close.
    *I'm completely against this. Really. I'm calling you*

*on the telephone every night at ten o'clock, at which time precisely you will be in your hotel room, ready for bed.*

K has invited me to Paris. He will be taking my picture, first for an important fashion magazine, and then maybe, if that goes well, for French *Vogue*. And now Mamma's standing there in the rain, on the sidewalk outside our building, a bulky bubble jacket, thick woolly socks, the red woolly hat on her head. The wind gusted.

Wait, she shouted.

Her socks were soaked in the slush. Wait.

She removed her hat, pulled her hair away from her face, as if she wanted to wipe this whole hideous day from the universe's archive of hideous days, and then she pulled the hat down over my head – *hard*.

You wear it more than me anyway, she said, and I don't want you to be cold in Paris.

I race into the kitchen and tear open the parcel we've collected from the post office.

Mamma comes in after me and sets the grocery bags down on the chair. The parcel contains a large pink seashell.

Hmm, Mamma says, turning the shell in her hands.

She reads the card. It's not from the American, it's not from Pappa, it's not from anyone we even know really, but from someone who wants to be known to us, or to Mamma, in any case.

Hmm, Mamma says again, crumpling the wrapping paper and dropping it into the bin under the sink. She starts to unpack the shopping.

What am I to do with a big pink seashell?

For some days the shell remains on the kitchen table. It's as big as a pike, Mamma says, though I'm not sure she knows what a pike looks like exactly. Eventually Mamma puts the shell aside on the windowsill, it's too big to be left on the kitchen table, too big for the windowsill too, but that's where it stays, a pike-sized seashell alongside all the other objects that have ended up on display there and whose stories I've forgotten – a rose-painted wooden bowl, a vase filled with ox-eye daisies, a bright red ceramic bird.

If you put your ear to the shell, you can hear the murmur of the ocean, Mamma says.

She cries —

　She laments —

　She locks herself in the bathroom, sits down naked on the cold blue tiles, with her knees drawn up under her chin —

　Three big white bath towels hang on golden pegs —

　*Crybaby* —


But before that. Before the crying. Before I lay in K's bed, in K's white sheets, in K's long pale arms, before the rush of desire that shook my body like a gust of wind, before I locked myself in his bathroom and sat down naked on the freezing-cold bathroom floor with my knees drawn up under my chin, before all that: it was a never-ending night, a night whose scope, nearly forty years on, I struggle to comprehend. Not only the scope, but more specifically the order of events. If I can find order, I'll find the girl. And what do I want with her? I don't know. *What do you want with her?* I don't know. That's the honest answer. To bury her, perhaps, or revive her, or something in between. What happened in Paris — and everything that came before and everything that came after – assumes the character of water. I remember and forget in glimpses.

The things I remember – the hotel with the virginal made-up bed and the manageress behind the reception desk, Claude saying *vite, vite, vite*, the big, bright studio and the girl with the Rubik's cube, K's address on a scrap of paper, the pitch-dark staircase leading up to K's apartment, first floor, second floor, third floor, K's white sheets, K's hands, K's tongue, K's rage, *fucking crybaby* – will not easily be placed in a specific order. I have to create order – because in a book (or a memory) one word must come before the other, the first sentence before the next. And yet – it wasn't like that, not exactly like that.
*What was it like then?*
I've already said. Like water, pool after pool after pool, shapeless. What happened first and what happened after that, and after that again. I'm not sure.

I'm jet-lagged, disorientated, the day never ends, there's no hour-by-hour, no one-thing-after-another. I'm lost in a strange city. So many years have passed since then. But now I'm here, back in K's apartment. He's pacing back and forth. He's smoking constantly, all kinds of things. It's late afternoon. It was Claude who dropped us off. K opened the entrance door, and I followed him up the stairs. He lives, he says, on the second floor. He apologizes for the unlit staircase, there's something wrong with the wiring. I ask if he can take me to my hotel. He shakes his head. No, not now. We're having dinner at Z's place. You're coming with me, he says, his face lighting up. We'll go in a while, in an hour or two.

But I'm hungry now. I try not to cry.

K offers me gin. We drink gin. He's got tonic and cocaine too. I accept the tonic. He puts his head in my lap. He tells me I'm beautiful in the light from the lamp posts outside the windows. My red hat is on the table. I've taken it off and put it back on many times. I don't know if it's true that I'm beautiful.

I try one more time.

Can you help me find the name of my hotel? And as an explanation of why I need to know: *My suitcase is there with all my things in it.*

I choose an exact time, an exact date: 8 p.m., 19 January 1983. I find the girl in a sumptuous apartment in the 7th arrondissement. She's by no means the first fourteen-, fifteen-, sixteen-, seventeen-year-old girl to have ascended the splendid spiral staircase to the first floor and walked through the door to be welcomed by Z, whose eyes appraise her in a glance, up, down, back, front. Claude is there, fat and perspiring, panting like a hungry dog. One beautiful young woman after another glides, ghost-like, over the creaky wood floor. Z embraces K, a kiss on each cheek, says something in French that I don't understand, and then he says: Come in, come in. Z – sporting a pair of bleached jeans, worn high above the hip and belted tightly at the waist – has curls like K, but Z's hair is dyed blond and glossy in a way that K's isn't. He doesn't look at me much that night, mainly just a long, cold stare when I leave the apartment an hour later with two older girls, before dinner is served.

The guests occupy a large corner sofa around an enormous enamel, bronze and glass coffee table. The girls have long legs. The men are old. I sit next to K. Everyone talks all at once, in loud voices. On the table is a bottle of gin and a bowl of peanuts. The girls are between five foot nine and six feet tall. I'm five foot five and a half. But Maxine, the modelling agent in New York, has said that as long as I'm agreeable and smart and work hard and do as she says she can make something out of what I have, which is, it's been said, *a cute little hourglass figure, a narrow waist and nice legs*. I'm sitting on the sofa in Z's magnificent apartment, thinking about K's head in my lap a couple of hours earlier. Can I take his hand? Would that be so totally wrong? Does it matter if everyone here knows that something is happening between K and me? K has never looked at me the way Claude and Z and the other men look at me, up and down, back and front, like I am a piece of cake. *A piece of sex*. K is forty-four, nearly forty-five. He likes to discuss film and music. K isn't disgusting, he doesn't wear leather pants drawn tightly together at the waist like Z, he doesn't proffer expensive watches from inside a grubby coat like Claude. My hunger makes me disorientated. My stomach churns. Of course you can't hold K's hand. What was it he said in the red jeep on the way here? *There's clearly something special between us, but you know, people jump to conclusions. It's best no one knows you were at my place this afternoon, okay?* Yes, of course, I nodded, I understand. And nothing has happened between us. I mean – he's barely touched me. This isn't that kind of story. K and I aren't like that. I drink the gin and tonic, Claude is the one mixing the drinks and he's given me one. Some of the girls disappear into one of the bathrooms and return giggling. I sip my drink, eat the peanuts. None of the other girls eats peanuts, but I can't stop. First one peanut. Then another. Then a handful. Then another handful. For a short moment, a few seconds, it's as if the salt of the peanuts and the tartness of the gin will quiet the hunger, calm the body. But the truth is, things are not going the right way. My belly rumbles. One of the tall girls looks at me and says in English: Do you want more nuts? There's more in the kitchen.

I shake my head.

The girl laughs.

And then everyone around the table goes quiet. Can they sense my disquiet?

Cheers, says K, and lifts his glass.

Cheers, says Z, in his parody of a French accent.

All but one of the girls lift their glasses. The one who doesn't is wearing a red blouse. Red like the poppy-patterned wallpaper in my bedroom when I was little, red like my father's bicycle. The light-headedness is more and more pronounced.

The girl in the red blouse perches on the edge of a straight-back chair. There isn't room for everyone on the corner sofa. Above the coffee table hangs an antique crystal chandelier with a thousand twinkling lights. *A thousand? Surely, you're exaggerating again.* The girl in the red blouse sits at some distance from everyone else, looking at K and me. She says nothing. Someone's put on Men at Work, playing the same track, 'Down Under', over and over, and when the other girls start dancing, the girl in the red blouse remains seated. I too stay where I am, visible and invisible at the same time, on the sofa next to K. Every time I look at the girl she frowns and shakes her head. Have I made her angry? Have I offended her? I want more peanuts, but now the bowl is empty. It's not clear to me when dinner will be. K sits next to me on the sofa but acts as if we don't know each other. He chats with Claude in French; now and then Claude goes completely quiet, stops speaking mid-sentence, to ogle the dancing girls. K grins. Not at the girls, K isn't interested in them, but at Claude ogling. It's nearly nine o'clock, in an hour I have to be back at my hotel, Mamma said she would call at ten. I take a breath. In, out. I won't be there at ten, she'll call and I won't be there, it won't happen.

*Fuck this*, says the girl in the red blouse. Her voice is loud. The tip of her nose is as red as her blouse. *This is bullshit!*

She speak English with a French accent: *Why doesn't someone say something?*

The girls stop dancing. One of them, the one who smiled at me earlier, fumbles with the controls and forgets to lift the stylus, trying to silence the music, scratching the record in the process. Z looks up and curses under his breath. One by one, the girls sit down on the sofa again and smile, like schoolgirls, which most of them are.

The girl in the red blouse shakes her head. She continues speaking, but in French now, pointing a finger at K and me. I don't understand what's being said, apart from when Claude offers her a cigarette and she tells him to shut up.

K shakes his head. K rolls his eyes. K groans. Z stares at the ceiling, more annoyed than anything else.

The girl who turned off the music, scratching Z's record, sits down beside me, on the armrest, and whispers in English that the girl in the red blouse is talking about me. K and me. Anyone can see what's going on here, she translates, anyone can fucking see, we all know the only reason you're in Paris and getting work is that K's sleeping with you, though why he's picked you is a total mystery, the girl says, embarrassed; she puts her arm around me, whispers that what she means is that you don't look like a model, you're not . . . tall . . . everyone here works like crazy, hoping to get a break, you know, runs from one go-see to the next with their stupid portfolios, and you're not . . . you're not . . .

The girl in the red blouse gets to her feet, all of her more than six-feet-tall Giacometti frame, the whole majesty of *Grande femme I, II, III* and *IV*, unfolds all at once, trembling, still speaking, but after some time interrupted by K, who says (whispers the translator girl) that the two of you are not sleeping together, of course you're not, *it's not because of me that she's here* . . . Is it true what he says? she asks quietly, I nod yes, it's true, yes, yes, yes, everything the girl in the red blouse says is a lie. Z gestures, as if to waft away a fly, and tells the girl in the red blouse to shut her mouth. Enough now, he says.

Many years later, while writing this, I read about the accusations of rape against Z. News stories are all over the Internet. He's old now. Over eighty. But his dyed hair is still fair. A camera team, all wearing masks because of the pandemic, approach him outside a restaurant where he's eating spaghetti and drinking wine with three other old men. The journalist asks if he'd care to comment on the accusations against him. One of Z's friends asks the journalist to leave. Z carries on eating and drinking. But then, when the journalist refuses to leave and instead begins asking one question after another about events that took place many decades ago, Z raises his hand and performs the same small gesture, as if to waft away a fly; I recognize it from that night in his apartment. Shut your mouth, he told the girl in the red blouse.

She gets to her feet immediately, turns crimson from the tip of her nose to her cheeks and brow.

You're all bastards, she says.

And then, to the girls on the sofa: Don't be whores.

And to me, in English – I remember her well, the red blouse, the long, delicate frame, the crimson face, I've never known if she wished me well or ill, if she spoke from a place of care or contempt – You have no business being here, get out, go home.

Mamma came up against a knot, a big one. I had many. My hair was full of them. She tried to unravel it without pulling out too much hair.

She had ears the size of seashells, hands that could unravel knots.
    She could draw a comb through my hair again and again and again without it hurting.

Now she's eighty-one, eighty-two, eighty-three, unable to drink her tea without rattling the china. Her hands tremble. It's because of her trembling, she says, that she can't use email or send text messages.
    I see her before me in a red Dior suit from 1970, with shiny, shoulder-length hair. She walks along the street.
    People turn to look at her.
    She says she's always felt left out, bony, invisible. It's hard to comprehend.

*

And she could tell me stories without reading from a book. She could sing too, not prettily, but I liked it. Whenever she had a new role on the stage or in a film, she had to learn all the words by heart. It was a big part of her preparation, learning by heart, and even though she was at home, on the sofa, or in bed, she was still at work.

Just like everyone who goes to the office, she said.

Who's going to the office?

Everyone who goes to the office, she repeated. What I mean is: I'm at work too, I'm working even though I'm at home. People don't realize.

Sometimes I'd help her learn her lines. It wasn't always effective. In fact she worked best without me. I would do things you're not supposed to do when helping an actor learn her lines. *I'd act the part.* For instance, if I was reading the male lover role, I would speak in a deep, seductive voice like I was actually a man.

You're not meant to be acting, Mamma said, you're meant to read the lines in your normal voice.

And so then I would read in my normal voice and follow the script closely to make sure she said her lines exactly as they appeared on the page.

No, Mamma, I'd interrupt, there's no *and*, it's just a comma.

Yes, but that's not important.

But it doesn't say *and*, I'd insist, and you said *and*. That's a mistake, Aren't I supposed to tell you when you make mistakes?

Mamma sighed.

If you keep interrupting all the time, we'll never get through.

Okay, so I'm *not* supposed to tell you, is that it?

No, of course you're supposed to tell me, but only if it's something important.

I watched her mouth. One eye on the words, the other on Mamma's mouth. I whispered to myself: Mamma's mouth exists.

Mamma was called Jenny in the new film, Mamma explained. In the scene that had to be learned by heart, my name was Anna, a girl of about my age, or maybe a couple of years older.

Mamma: You must try to forgive me.
Me: I don't know what you mean.
The script says: *The distance, the insurmountable distance. Jenny is mute and beaten.*
Mamma, who is neither mute nor beaten, has told me not to bother about the bits between the lines, the stage directions, the instructions to the actors. That's not meant to be read aloud, she said. Forget about that. She took a deep breath.
Mamma: Are you going back to camp today?
Me: There's a train in an hour.

Mamma: Do you have enough money?

Me: Yes thanks.

Mamma: Are you all right?

I looked up from the script.

But Mamma, I said, that's not what it says.

What?

It doesn't say, *Are you all right?* It says, *Are you all having a nice time?* That's two different things.

Mamma sighed and looked at something on the ceiling.

*Mute and beaten?*

*The distance, the insurmountable distance?*

Mamma sighed again and said, Okay, my sweet, we'll try again, shall we?

I nodded.

Mamma: You must try to forgive me.

Me: I don't know what you mean.


When we were tired and lay next to each other in her big bed with the golden bedposts and she thought I was sleeping, I would squeeze my eyes shut but leave a little slit through which to look at her, catching glimpses. She'd read her script, or a book, or watch TV. I'd whisper quietly to myself: Her eyes exist. Her cheeks exist. Her mouth (lips slightly apart, rather slack, because they didn't know they were being looked at) exists. Her hair. Her eyebrows. Her brow. All of her exists. Her hands, long and cool.

Sometimes, when I was a child and Mamma was young, we pretended we were magpies. We didn't have names. We referred to each other only as Magpie One and Magpie Two, though which of us was which wasn't important. We flapped around town or hopped about in the park while talking about ordinary things. We didn't put on airs, but spoke in our normal voices.

Mamma calls from the theatre and says her friend has had a baby and that she's the godmother.

You can come and say hello tomorrow, she tells me from the payphone outside her dressing room, but only if you're feeling better. It's important the baby doesn't catch anything.

Congratulations on your new god-baby, I say.

Thanks, she says. And it's called a godchild.

Did it hurt? I ask.

I imagine it did a bit, she says.

When you had me, I mean.

I don't think it hurt at all, she says, but I remember screaming a few times for the sake of appearances. I didn't want the doctor to think I was strange.

Oh? Wow.

It was the happiest day in my life – when you came into the world.

Okay.

Ever since you were born, I've been afraid of losing you.

Okay.

See you tomorrow?

Okay. Yes. Shall we hang up now?

Yes – no, wait, I'll see you tonight when I get home after the show, but you'll be asleep then.


The baby, who hasn't yet been given a name, lies tucked up next to Mamma's friend in a big white hospital bed. Mamma is already there and sits on the edge of the bed with her long hair in a ponytail.


My cold makes me feel heavy and drowsy. I'm warm and clammy too, maybe I'm running a temperature. I place a finger cautiously under my nose to prevent a sneeze. It's a trick actors use. Actors have to practise not sneezing when they're standing in the wings waiting to make an entrance – otherwise the audience will hear, and the sneeze will ruin the performance.


I've stayed home from school, though without telling Mamma, who went out early. I've taken a couple of aspirins and put some make-up on so no one at the hospital can tell that I'm ill. All these – *tricks*. I know thousands of them.


Mamma's friend has been practising her breastfeeding (apparently this too is something that has to be practised); some milk dribbles from her breasts, they're not covered up, they look more alive than the baby. She tucks the breasts back inside her dressing gown. Although my nose is blocked, I still sense the cloying smell of her milk, and of pork chops. Perhaps all new mothers are given meat to eat for lunch. Didn't I read somewhere, or hear someone say, that women who've just given birth need to eat a lot of meat? I breathe in, then out. Hi, I say. There are two other women sharing the room. They haven't got their babies with them. It's important for mothers to rest after giving birth. Mamma's friend looks up, smiles and says hi. The other women in the room look up, smile and say hi. Mamma looks up too, but she doesn't smile and she doesn't say hi. No words escape Mamma's mouth. The whole of Mamma just sits there on the edge of the bed, looks at me and is completely silent.

But before all that, before I took the tram to the hospital, I went into my mother's room and sat down at her dressing table with its glass top and its three-sided mirror. I could see my face from three different angles. I had faces I never knew I had.

There's an ugliness in our family's faces, Mamma said once.

I smeared white foundation all over my face. Foundation is supposed to be brown, hence the Norwegian *brunkrem*, but the one Mamma has on her dressing table makes you pale as a ghost; it says *ivory* on the bottle.

\*

High up on the living-room wall in our apartment in Oslo there hangs a woman's face, a Japanese theatre mask.

*Noh*, said Mamma.

Mamma's hands unravel knots and unpack the mask from its silk paper. It must be hung up high, she says. Mamma pulled a chair up to the wall, stepped up on top of it and hammered the nails through the wallpaper. The nails bent or dropped to the floor. It took a long time. Mamma hammered and hammered.

Mamma said that some masks are a sign of bad luck and some are a sign of good luck, and this one was a sign of good luck. It's possible she was wrong.

It's a valuable mask, she said, made from cypress and crushed seashells, hand-painted by the artist.

That day at the hospital with ivory-white foundation on my face, I looked very Noh. The baby mustn't catch cold, Mamma said several times. The baby was forty-two hours old; the only thing it could do, as far as I could see, was to stick out its tongue. Mamma's friend was forty-two *years* old and strictly speaking too old to have a baby. But I didn't say so out loud. I was generally careful about saying things out loud. Often things came out all wrong. I sat down gently next to Mamma on the edge of the bed and took the baby's hand in mine. It was no bigger than a man's big toe.

Mamma said: Hasn't she got lovely eyes, aren't they lovely?
    She always spoke this way. *Eyes. Lovely.* Light from the big window spilled on to the hospital bed, the two women and Mamma's god-baby.
    What have you done to your face, said Mamma.
    I shook my head.
    Are you wearing make-up? she said. You know I've forbidden it. Have you been using my make-up?
    Mamma spat on her fingers, *ptui, ptui,* and began to rub. First my cheeks, then under my eyes. Don't spit, I said. Urgh. It's disgusting.
    You can't go around looking like that, said Mamma. *Ptui!*
    She spat on her fingers again and carried on rubbing.
    If the baby's face ever gets dirty and you wipe it with spit, I'm going to protect her, I said, protect her from you two.
    Mamma and her friend laughed – and I laughed then too.
    I looked at the baby. She was asleep with her tongue out. Some people say a child chooses its parents. I'm not sure. That's a big responsibility to give to a child.

\*

When does it actually start, the job of managing – to live, to speak, to memorize, to comprehend? Mamma's friend placed the baby carefully in Mamma's arms.

I have to go to the bathroom, she said. Can you look after her for a minute? And then she climbed out of bed and walked, waddled, wobbled out of the room.

Mamma and I sat very still on the edge of the bed, looking at the baby. After a moment, Mamma put her forehead to mine.

I think you're running a temperature, she said.

No, I said with a shake of my head.

I'm just very tired, I said, and started to cry.


Many years later I read an article about how important the very first hour is for a baby – about all the work the newborn has to do. Everything happens between zero and one. This particular baby had lived for forty-two hours when I held her hand. I had no idea she was already an old soul. First crying, the article said, then finding the mother's breast, then resting, then waking up, then moving the limbs and the head, then resting again, then sucking, then sleeping.


And every time I see a girl walking up and down the street while talking to herself in a low and determined voice, I want to stretch out a hand, stroke her brow, ask, *Is everything all right, are you lost, can I help you*, only I don't, because it's by no means certain she will want that. I know, of course, that if a person walks in their sleep, one must take care not to wake them. If someone suffers an attack (anxiety, epilepsy), you mustn't try to force them out of it.

I've never been much good at distinguishing between what happened and what *may have* happened. The contours are blurred, and Mamma's face is a big white cloud over it all. Long before I turned sixteen – long before winter 1983 in Paris – I dreamed I was all four of my dolls at the same time and that our hearts ticked, ticked, ticked, like clocks in an old clockmaker's shop. All that ticking made me light-headed. That might be what I remember best from when I was a little girl. I was light-headed all the time. I fainted often. At school. At ballet class. I fell. And again. Fell. And again. Fell. As if it were some eternal choreography. Grazes and scrapes. Bumps on my forehead and skull, sprained limbs. Eventually I learned how to fall safely. Perhaps *you* helped me with that. Mamma used to say an angel was watching over me. Did she say so because she sensed you were near? Did she know you existed, and that you were hers? What I remember most clearly from that time – when I used to faint – isn't the bumps and bruises, but my astonishment at having been gone. Not for long, but long enough not to have existed.

There weren't many things I was certain of when I was little, but one thing I knew for sure was that once I turned sixteen, everything would be all right. The embarrassments of childhood would be overturned. All I had to do was look at Mamma. The way she walked from room to room and the eyes that followed her. Mamma noticed those looks and allowed herself to be looked at. Anyone who caught a glimpse of her was captivated by her beauty, gripped by the desire to kiss her, or hit her, or both.

I was eight, nine, ten, eleven, twelve, thirteen years old and had a body that captivated no one.

Mamma's body was much more real to me than my own. Nothing about it escaped me. Her soft tummy in which I could bury my face, her pale skin, the freckles on her head and shoulders, her long strawberry-blonde hair. I would never get to be like her. I had none of her softness. I was small and skinny, there wasn't a single place on my body where another person could rest their head. So yes, I needed something more than this collection of bones, thin pale hair, long fingers and big lips that added up to me and nothing more than me.

For a while, you were my secret sister, you were real, not embryonic and formless as you are now.

I was still a child and in need of protection; I couldn't just go out into the world and get myself a job and a roof over my head. Can I live here? No, you're a child and must live at home. Can I work here? No, you're a child and must go to school. You can't hide the fact that you're a child. You wish you could. You wish you were older – someone who would say, unblinking, don't touch me like that, don't touch me like that, only you're thirteen and don't know how to do anything.

Go home, little girl. The grown-up world isn't ready for you yet.

Your body is a hindrance even at its most youthful and becoming. At thirteen, no one bothers to look at you, though. Youthful and becoming isn't for a few years yet. For the time being, your body is a spindly, childish thing.

A party is held in the Oslo apartment. Mamma is the hostess. A guest grabs hold of my arm, grips me tight and whispers in my ear (he's so close I can hear the cracks on his vocal chords), You'll be gorgeous one day, I can tell by your bum.

    How do you mean? I ask.

    Because you already have a nice bum, he answers.

    The man is known as the Saddler because of his leathery skin.

    Men who adore women, he says, can be divided into two categories, those who like breasts and those who like bums, and I, he says, am a bum man.

I serve red punch from a big glass bowl. My job, for which I'm paid twenty kroner, is to stand at a small table and ladle punch into people's glasses. Mamma crosses the floor and smells ravishing. I don't know if it's her hair or her hands or her throat or her laughter that always smells so good. If you fill some glasses and put them on a tray, you can go around and offer them to the guests, she says, rather than just waiting for them to come to you. *Breathless* is the word. There's something breathless about the way Mamma moves past my little table. I do as she says, and it's while I'm going around the room with my tray full of clinking glasses that the Saddler grabs me by the arm, grips me tight and whispers in my ear. The punch sloshes precariously, but not a drop is spilled. You'll take time yet, he says, two years perhaps, three at the most, but I can already tell. He inhales me like I am a drink. Though not punch, that's not what he wants. He wrinkles his nose and asks if my mother's got anything better to offer. A whisky, not this watery swill. It's the first time a man has looked at me and told me what he sees. I move carefully, making my way across the floor, there are people everywhere, some of whom I recognize, others I've never seen before. The lights have been dimmed and Mamma has put a record on, 'Killing Me Softly' by Roberta Flack. She loves that record. She's wearing her long plum-coloured dress, the one she calls her kaftan. I balance my tray of drinks on a raised hand like a proper waitress, I know the Saddler is watching me, and I turn and smile at him. I remember to close my mouth. A childish smile would ruin everything.

But then: fourteen. Mamma and I have been dividing our time between the USA and Norway for some years, first here, then there, it's Mamma's work that decides where we live and now we're back in New York. And I *am not* living in a yellow house with two Swedish babysitters in the fucking middle of nowhere like last time. Mamma and I live in the same city, in the same shadowy apartment, in a West Side building with a green canopy over the entrance.

You and I –

You and I have promised each other we'll be together for ever, but now that I'm fourteen and living in New York you don't appear as often as before. I'm too old to have invisible sisters. But one day you came anyway, into my room, sat down next to me on my bed and said: Be quiet and listen.

 I put a finger to my lips. Like this?

 Yes, you said. That's it. If you're quiet and listen and pay attention to everything that's happening around you, you'll know how to stay out of harm's way. Try to be the girl on whom nothing is lost.

Yes.

You'll know what's happening *before* it happens, and then you'll be able to do something about it.

Yes.

Do you know what the Mountain Code is?

Yes.

The thing is: someone came up with these rules to ensure people's safety when hiking, skiing and walking in the mountains.

But we're not in the mountains, we're in New York.

I lay down on the bed and put my head in your lap.

What I'm trying to say, you said, leaning over me, I could almost feel your breath on my lips, what I'm trying to say is that the rules for how you walk in the mountains can just as well apply to how you walk in the world.

I looked up.

You sat there startlingly alive, entirely distinct from me.

I shook my head.

What I mean is, you said, it might be useful to think of danger like different kinds of weather. It's something you have to prepare for!

Okay.

What I'm trying to tell you is that if you pay attention and always come prepared, things will probably turn out fine.

In November 2019, global temperatures had risen to nearly one degree Celsius above average.
*Not just on land*, Eva texted. *It's the oceans too.*
Soon it would be Christmas and an online article tells the story of a man who'd been admitted to hospital suffering from a new kind of virus.
Then another text came from Eva:
*It's the warmest November on record.*


But before that, long before Eva sent me texts about November temperatures far exceeding the norm, Klaus Barbie, the war criminal, the Butcher of Lyon, was arrested in Bolivia and extradited to France. It is January 1983 in Paris. The French defence secretary, Charles Hernu, who will be forced to step down two years later after the bombing of the Greenpeace ship *Rainbow Warrior*, commented on Barbie's capture, stating: *How could one not hope that the hands of justice would catch hold at last of those responsible for atrocious crimes.* The sixteen-year-old girl has her mind on different matters altogether, though she did see the arrest on the television news before leaving New York. Now she's seated on the sofa in the spectacular apartment belonging to Z. His past will also catch up with him one day, when ten or so women accuse him of sexual abuse, rape and trafficking. It has not occurred to him, however, that such a thing as *the hands of justice* will concern themselves with him. It occurs to no one. Not to the men, not to the girls. This is a different time.

I remember the girl who translated from French to English, the way she balanced herself on the sofa's armrest, the way she leaned into me, put a thin arm around my shoulder and whispered in my ear:

*Is it true you're sleeping with K?*

*No.*

*Is it true he's photographing you for French* Vogue*?*

*No, or rather, I don't know . . . maybe, if things go well tomorrow.*

K takes no notice of me. Someone puts 'Down Under' on again.

No, not that, Z cries out, and does that thing with his hand, the wafting gesture, not that again.

He gets to his feet slowly, and in the manner of a much older man, saunters over to his stereo to change the record.

Claude spreads his legs in the big armchair and runs a hand through his hair. The translator girl leans towards me and whispers: Let's go!

She smiles.

I look up at her. Go? Where?

She gives a nod to one of the other girls, who nods back.

The other girl has a cropped pixie-cut like Mia Farrow in *Rosemary's Baby*. K has been eying her.

Out, says the translator girl, out somewhere. But first back to ours, yes? You probably want to change?

I'm not sure.

I look at K, who sits with his back to me.

The other girl, the translator's friend, the one I call Mia, gets to her feet and smiles at Z, who strokes her bottom. She laughs and pecks his cheek.

We're leaving, the translator girl says. I stand up.

K turns around.

Where are you going? he says quietly.

I'm going out, I'm going with . . .

She's coming with us, says the translator girl, and smiles at K.

Are you sure about that? K says, though it's unclear whether he's talking to her or to me.

She's quite sure, yes, aren't you? the translator girl asks.

K smiles.

Does she think she can find her way in Paris all alone? As far as I know she only just flew in from New York today.

We'll look after her, says the translator girl.

Mia comes up and takes my hand. The two girls tower over me.

We're taking her with us now, Mia says to K.

Z lifts his gaze and looks at me for the second time that night. I offer him a big smile. K has told me it's important Z likes what he sees. Important for my future. Z gives a hard, cold laugh – and never looks at me again.

Late evening at the translator girl's place. Mia lives here too. And three other girls, but they're not home. It's 11 p.m. There are clothes everywhere. The tiles in the bathroom are dirty-white, washed articles of clothing have been hung to dry on a line strung out above the bathtub, and in the sink there's mascara, lipstick, eyeshadow, blush, highlighter.

I'll do your make-up, the translator girl says.

I'll lend you some clothes as well, she adds, rummaging through a pile on one of the beds.

Mia has produced a bottle of gin and some tonic water; she sits down at the table and lights a cigarette. Her short hair lends her an air of unreachability.

I don't suppose —

A wave of dizziness and nausea comes over me as I take a sip from the glass the translator girl has handed me. My head has somehow loosened from my body. It feels odd.

I don't suppose you've got some bread or a biscuit or something?

Mia gets up with her cigarette in her mouth, glides across the floor to the untidy worktop, finds a baguette in a paper bag and cuts it up into slices. She takes a banana from the fridge, turns and says: I can make you some bread with banana on top. I grew up with my grandmother and she always gave me bread and banana, proper bread though, not a fucking baguette, slabs like doorsteps, always still warm from the bakery. She's so proud of me. Here I am in Paris working as a model with all the greatest photographers, earning my own money.

She puts a plate out in front of me, with the bread and banana. Working every day, you understand, she says, just trying to get a break. The cigarette dangles from her lip. She must be nearly two metres tall.

Eat this, you won't feel so dizzy.

I eat. The baguette is crusty and cold, the banana overripe. It's delicious.

Thank you, I say, and I'm sorry.

No need to say sorry, the translator girl quips. I think what you need is some lipstick. And a change of dress.

How about this, she says, it's like silk, and short enough to show off your legs. You've got nice legs, you should show them off more.


Mia sits down at the table again and lights another cigarette.

The translator girl ushers me out to the bathroom with her.

If you just need a pee you can do it here, she says,

indicating the bidet. Anything more and you'll need the key, the toilet's in the corridor.

I'm all right . . .

I love doing other girls' make-up, the translator girl says.

I sit down on the edge of the bidet. She holds my chin as she smears foundation on my face.

Did you have one of those big doll's heads when you were little, with long hair you could style in different hairdos, that came with make-up and a hairbrush?

The big head without the body, I say.

I always wanted one of those dolls, she says, emphasizing each word, but wait and see what I'm going to do with you! First the eyes, then the lips, then the hair.

*Voilà*, she says after twenty minutes, and now it's almost midnight. She tells me to stand up and look in the mirror.

My eyes are sooty, my mouth a big red apple. I think maybe it's a bit much, I say.

The translator girl says it's dark where we're going, so our make-up needs to be heavy.

Everything depends on whether it's day or night, dark or light, she says.

I nod. Okay, yes, it's nice, I like it.

She throws her arms around me and whispers: We can be friends if you want. You and me. Do you want to? Tell me you do.

The nightclub is big, packed, completely dark, hot.

No, not completely *dark*, says the girl who used to be me. If you look closely you can see me.

The heat is like a wall, but the darkness is shattered by the lights, green, red, violet, that sweep across the faces, the bodies.

You can see me, can't you?

A drunk man tries to tear off my dress, the one I borrowed from the translator girl. I want to see you naked, he says, I want to see you naked on the dance floor.

*Take it off, take it off.*

Another man appears. He's in a dark suit too. For a moment I think this second man is going to punch the first, he looks so determined, but then he steps up behind me, right up against my spine, reaches his hand between my legs and says into my ear, in English: *You're wet.*

I shake my head.

I push him away, push them both away, press a path through the bodies, through the lights, the music, to Mia and the translator girl, who are sitting with some people they know, men and women they've met here, met a long time ago, met after I disappeared on to the dance floor. Their friends have a big table – they have chairs, champagne, cigarettes, cocaine, dark suits, shirts, ties, long legs, laughter, jewellery.

The two men come after me. Everyone knows each other. They exchange greetings across the table. They greet Mia. They greet the translator girl.

The first man looks at me and grins, then says loudly to anyone who'll listen: She's wet. Everyone laughs. Wet and ready. *He's wrong.* I look at the men and women, the girls around the table. *I'm not . . .* Mia lights a cigarette, leans across and says in a whisper that everyone can hear:

*Stupid little girl, if you can't handle people touching you, you shouldn't be here.*

I can handle it, I say.


Outside, it's night, snowing. My coat is blue with a belt tied around the waist. My woolly hat is red. I don't know where I am. I came with the girls and thought I'd be leaving with them too. I leaned across the table and asked the translator girl if we could go now, if she'd leave with me, if we could go back to her apartment together, maybe I could stay the night, but the music was pounding, she shook her head and laughed, I can't hear what you're saying, she said, waving her arms to indicate that it was impossible to hear anything above the music, the laughter, the lights and the smoke. I got up. I put my coat on. As I stepped past her, she took hold of my wrist, stood up and threw her arms around me. Then she sat down again.

I walk along the pavement. First one way, then the other. I don't know where I am.

Shall I tell you what happened that January night in Paris – in 1983?
　I got lost.
　I couldn't remember the address of the hotel or what it was called. *A manageress. A big gilded key. Cats everywhere, in the reception area, on the carpeted stairs. A bed made up ready on the second floor.* I'd written K's address down on a scrap of paper. He tore a page out of a book, a novel, I think, I don't know which, and told me to write down his address and phone number.

So, although passers-by, dog-walkers and other night wanderers wanted to help me, no one could, *have you any idea at all where you want to go*, what was I supposed to answer, *no, I don't know*, and then I met the man who persisted, the man with the red scarf. He couldn't speak English and I couldn't speak French, but he didn't just leave me like all the others. He babbled and babbled and shook his head. I babbled too, and shook my head.

*

I think he really wanted to help.

Eventually, I found the scrap of paper with K's address on it in my coat pocket, and then, after saying something along the lines of *why didn't you show me this to begin with*, he walked me all the way to the front door.

Something occurred to me today. I want to tell you about calm. It comes as unexpectedly as joy, or sleep when you thought you couldn't sleep, or laughter, or like the girl you didn't know was nearby, who runs up and down the stairs, knocking on all the doors and asking for you. Breathing doesn't always help. It's by no means certain that you'll be able to calm yourself down with deep belly breaths and long exhalations just because you know that's what you're supposed to do. The dog is a year older now. He can't go on for ever. That's what I want. For him to live longer. His legs are thin and stiff, it's a clatter of bones every time he gets up or lies down beside me in the grass. We go for walks every day. His black coat shines. The coat says a lot about how a dog is doing, and his coat is fine. We can't find shade anywhere. Not even beneath the elm trees. Nothing is like before, when he and I would go for walks without a thought as to how long we might be gone, but now he wants to sniff at everything, he doesn't want to miss a single smell in his fourteenth year. At home, in the cool apartment where the dog and I live with my husband and Eva, I fill his bowl with water and put it down on the floor. He lowers his head and drinks.

\*

If you'd been alive, if you'd been real, we could have stood there together and listened to the sound of the dog drinking water. He laps it up, *thlup, thlup, thlup.* It's the most beautiful sound I know, and completely untranslatable.

The red woolly hat itches. K takes a step towards me and snatches it from my head, tosses it on to the table by the window. A round table and two chairs. It's where he eats breakfast in the mornings, and now, instead of a vase of red poppies, my woolly hat is on it, looking stupid. He sits down on one of the chairs. He looks at his watch. Reaches his arm out and shows me the face.

What does it say? he asks.

I lean forward and look.

Half past two, I say.

Half past two *in the morning*, he says.

I'm standing on the wooden floor with my blue coat done up at the waist.

Don't you think it's a bit late to be turning up and ringing the doorbell?

Yes, I do.

He draws me towards him.

Half past two, he says.

I put my arms around his neck.

I couldn't find my hotel and I can't remember what it's called, but I had your address on the scrap of paper in my pocket. I try to give it to him.

K fidgets with a piece of red fluff on my coat collar.

Perhaps you should have stayed with me instead of flouncing off.

I didn't flounce off.

He continues to fidget.

Ah, he says, let's look at what happened. We were at Z's place. I wanted to drive you home. To your hotel. But you said you'd rather go with the girls. You said you could look after yourself.

I was wrong, I said. I'm sorry to have woken you up.

K looks at me and smiles. He reaches for the belt of my coat and unties it slowly.

There's nothing left of the sixteen-year-old in the body I walk around in today, only some scarring under my breasts after a case of sunburn, red-brown flecks, as if that prehistoric bird had walked about on me. Sometimes I imagine you were that bird. Big and red. That the pressure I sense, the trembling, the soaring, is you. Strong winds, heat and drought have given new life to the forest fires in Australia. More than one million creatures have perished there. In every picture the Australian sky is orange.

It's January 2020, thirty-seven years after I went to Paris to be photographed by K. I'm sure he doesn't remember me. What if I sent him an email? Dear K. Remember me? The girl with the bare shoulders and the long earrings? Do you still have the photograph you took of me?

The park sits like a great big kneecap in the landscape, surrounded by pale yellow apartment buildings, hemmed in by Agathe Grøndahls Street to the north, Johan

Svendsens Street to the southeast, Hegermanns Street to the south and Per Kvibergs Street to the west. The tall, bare deciduous trees look like reflections in water — as if what I'm seeing are reflections rather than the trees themselves. There's something upside-downish about the whole park. I've often thought about counting the trees in it, and have sometimes tried, one, two, three, four, but after a while my thoughts turn to something else and I have to start again. The January sunsets are so spectacular here that people come flocking to see them. Anyone would think they were on the Isle of Skye in Scotland or at Langhammars on Fårö or at the Taj Mahal in India, all celebrated for their sunsets, but we're here, in Oslo, in the Torshov district, in the uncelebrated upside-down park that takes its name from the neighbourhood. I'll often stand at the kitchen window and watch people as they flock to see the glowing, smouldering winter sun like a child's feverish cheek there in the sky, a big cheek, a giant's cheek, a giant child's feverish cheek. It looks hot, but it's only January, and outside it is cold and soon completely dark.

You – yes, *you, you, you* – you sit in my heart, my throat, my bones, my belly, a big red bird with fiery yellow feathers, pecking and pecking. You turned up in September and now it's spring. March, April.

Every day – on the Internet, on TV – new images of empty streets, empty apart from the animals: a raccoon in New York, a jackal in Tel Aviv, a deer in Nara, a sea lion in Buenos Aires. Eva closes her bedroom door each morning and switches the computer on.

I search for the word *distance*. An article on the *Miami Herald* website advises: *If, despite your better judgement, you stop to speak to someone on the street, please remember always to keep your distance. Imagine, if you will, that there is a large alligator between you and everyone else at all times.*

I picture alligators in the streets.

I measure everything in alligators.

The same news article says: *Don't touch your face.*

I count the trees in the park, but give up after eleven, twelve, thirteen –

I go online and count instead the numbers of infected, the sick and the dead.

Eva comes home from a walk, her lips as red as her Dr. Martens. I can't tell her when all this is going to be over, when the schools are going to reopen.

She puts her head in her hands and weeps.

It's so unreal, she says.

*Go to her.*

My voice is much harsher, much stiffer than I'd anticipated.

Eva, I say, don't touch your face.

Once a week Mamma emails me a handwritten shopping list. Which is to say: Mamma can't do anything on the Internet, so we've set up a system whereby she sends me her list by fax, which, through a complicated computer program, turns up in my inbox as an email. I then order her items online.

Yoghurt, tinned stew, bread, Coca-cola, chocolate, melon, noodles, soap, rice.

I translate the shopping list into English, log on to the account I've created for her, and order the items. A few hours later, concluding the ritual, the things are delivered to her door in Massachusetts.


Mamma writes *a cake of soap* rather than *soap*. She'll write *beautiful penmanship* rather than *beautiful handwriting*. And she'll write *young girls* or *little girls* rather than just *girls*.


I lean closer to review her latest list, I can tell that her hand trembles more than before, and that she's taken time to write each item down neatly, in her most, yes, beautiful penmanship. Sometimes she adds a little drawing, of a girl walking her dog, for instance, or two girls sitting on a fence singing a song.

Over the phone she asks me what I'm writing; my answers are more often than not evasive. Or maybe I say I'm writing about a photo from 1983. What photo? she says. A photo someone took of me, I say. In Paris, you mean, she says. Yes, I say. And then she says, *But I didn't want you to go.* No, I say, you didn't.

She moves from room to room in the big house, or else she sits on a chair in front of the kitchen window looking out at the red maple tree.
    It must be a hundred years old, she says.

Another time on the phone: Hello, Mamma, are you there?
    I think I've locked myself out, she cries.
    Have you forgotten your key?
    No, I had to bring the groceries in and then I got locked out.
    I hear her breathing. Across the sea from Gloucester to Torshov.
    Hello, hello, she calls out, not to me this time but to her spouse, who is somewhere inside the house. He

can't hear her calling. The house, as she's described it to me, is a labyrinth of rooms and corridors and staircases. She likes the kitchen the best, and the maple tree outside.

Come and let me in, she calls out. Please, I'm locked out, you've got to let me in. Please.

Please.


A third time: I vacuum, says Mamma, I unpack the groceries, cook the food, set the table and do the dishes. Every day I'm afraid. Wash your hands, I say to my spouse, remember your mask, you can't go outside without a mask. He doesn't always listen to me, if you know what I mean. I hadn't imagined life would end like this.

Life doesn't end like this.

We don't know that, she says. It can easily end like this.


I haven't told her that she has another, that there are two of us, and that you've come back after having been gone for decades.


When a child is born, lots of things happen. The most important, which we almost never think about, is that during the first hour, the child, zero months, zero days, zero hours old, has to establish a new and independent relationship to gravity. For nine months it has floated. And now it can't any more. All this is hard work.


Sometimes you'll sit on the windowsill and pretend you're our mother. You say: I gave birth to both of you. One of you stayed, the other went away.

Spring 1982, a few months before my sixteenth birthday. I'm living in Norway, in the fifth form at Majorstuen School. Eirik, who will graduate from sixth-form college in a few weeks, is eighteen. He lies next to me in the narrow top bunk in the summer-house annex. He asks me quietly if this is my first time. I tell him yes.

The sun's up all night and the guests stay well into the morning. Some of the boys, Eirik included, have their licence, he has borrowed a car and can drive back to Oslo. The others catch the train. When everyone's gone, Heidi and I tidy and clean up as best we can after a party we weren't allowed to have. *The art of tidying up.* The five-year-old tidies up her toys, the ten-year-old tidies up, makes nice after her tantrums, the fifteen-year-old tidies up after an unpermitted party at her mother's summer house, the nineteen-year-old tidies up after long nights spent studying for exams, nights of coffee cups, ashtrays, books, papers, the twenty-four-year-old tidies up her son's toys, the twenty-nine-year-old divorcee tidies up the boxes in the attic now that she's moved into a new place with her son, Ola, and is working on her first book.

It's here, in the attic, that she finds the photograph K took of her in Paris, tucked between the pages of a white wire-bound notebook with nothing written in it. The photo shows her with bare shoulders and long earrings. She stares at it for a moment before closing the book and putting it back into the box. I think that was the last time she saw the photo. I've looked for it, am looking for it now as I write this, but it must have got lost during a move, either then, when I was almost thirty, twenty-five years or so ago, or later, during another move.

As I get older I appreciate the act of tidying up more and more, especially washing, hanging, ironing and folding clothes. I wonder sometimes if my fondness for housework makes me less of an art monster – an expression I've borrowed from the American author Jenny Offill, who in her novel *Dept. of Speculation* writes:

> My plan was to never get married. I was going to be an art monster instead. Women almost never become art monsters because art monsters only concern themselves with art, never mundane things. Nabokov didn't even fold his own umbrella. Vera licked his stamps for him.

The writing day inevitably begins with me draping newly washed sheets and duvet covers over the doors while thinking about my father, who clearly *was* an art monster. My father would never have got up one morning to do the laundry. It would never have occurred to him, as it does to me, to start a work day by hanging wet sheets out to dry – and he would never have allowed them to be draped over doors. He didn't even want to *see* a wet sheet. When I was little, at Hammars, he had a separate laundry room built, with a washing machine and an airing cupboard, and anyway it was always women (lovers, wives, housekeepers) who did the housework for him. And of course, everything had to be neat and tidy, spotless, everything in its place, the duster couldn't be left on the windowsill, the kitchen couldn't look like someone had been cooking in it when dinner was served at six o'clock by Mamma, for instance, when she was living with him. *Oh, I hate this house! It seems there is nothing that can be done to make it pretty!* Mrs G. says in Simone de Beauvoir's *The Second Sex*, and now the girl who is soon to turn sixteen, soon to go back to New York, soon to be discovered by K in an elevator, soon to go to Paris, is tidying up. All these things will happen in only a few months – the elevator, K, Paris – but she doesn't know that. What she knows is that she must tidy up every trace of the party, the bottles, the crisp bags, the cigarette butts. This is a different kind of housework from the kind Mrs G. performs day in, day out, the fifteen-year-old isn't doing it to make the house pretty, she doesn't think much at all about whether her mother's house is pretty, she thinks about whether *she* — the fifteen-year-old girl — is pretty. She's tidying up so that her mother won't suspect there's been a party and be angry.

I once wrote that my mother and father needed a wife to look after them — someone who could cook their meals, tidy their mess, answer their letters, tuck them in at bedtime. The girl who will soon be sixteen tidies up in order to conceal a lie. She promised she wouldn't have a party, and when her mother asks, she says that of course she didn't have a party. Heidi has stayed behind. Heidi helps her tidy up. It takes all morning. When they're finished, when we're finished, we lie down on our separate towels in the sun. We lie next to each other with a cassette player between us. Now and then Heidi gets up, she's the restless one, and starts to dance. Heidi dances on the smooth coastal rock, singing 'I Love Rock 'n' Roll', intermittently sucking an ice lolly. When she lies down again, I tell her I've slept with Eirik. I think we fall into a slumber then, made drowsy by the sleepless night, the alcohol, the sun. I've always been pale. Thin-skinned. Transparent, almost. You could see the veins under the skin of my hands, light blue, as if they were lungs. Even back then I had the hands of an old woman.

Evening comes and Mamma too, she brings bags full of groceries from the shop and intends to make a late dinner, it's already eight or nine o'clock. Mamma doesn't notice that the house is tidy, nor does she notice that there's been a party; her light blue eyes fixed on me, she says, *Oh, but look at you, have you been in the sun all day, you're bright red, you know we can't do that, our skin is too delicate.* Of course I know that Mamma has to stay out of the sun. And then it goes without saying that I have to stay out of the sun too. Mamma and I have similar first names – that is, my name is actually Karin, after my father's mother, but I don't go by that name. Most people call me something else. And when it comes to the sun, Mamma has been adamant about staying out of it year after year. Mamma in her long, thin dresses and dark sunglasses. Mamma who always seeks out the shade. *No, no, no, I won't sit in the sun. Not even for the briefest moment will I sit in the sun.* Summer after summer, Mamma's girlfriends come to the summer house and sip white wine and sunbathe on the smooth rocks at the shore in their bikinis, working up gorgeous tans, while Mamma sits on a bench in the shade, watching them from under her big black sun hat.

Sunburnt girl. Fifteen, almost sixteen. No longer a virgin. Her skin inflamed and tender to the touch, it doesn't help to apply oils and potions, it doesn't help to place cool cloths on her face and shoulders. She showers in cold water, she swims in the ocean, showers again, but her skin feels like a burning sock. That night, after a thousand cold showers and a thousand applications of magic concoctions, I want to lie close to Heidi, only it still hurts too much. My skin is hot, not exactly like a fever, but similar.

A few days later, a week, a fortnight, my whole chest blisters and the school nurse says I've got second-degree burns.

It's dangerous to lie in the sun all day, the nurse says. I know, I say, and resist the urge to tell her about Mamma sitting on her bench in the shade under her big black sun hat.

After a few more weeks, the skin begins to peel.


Eirik and I are together again in my bedroom in Mamma's Oslo apartment. He's had two wisdom teeth extracted. His jaw is swollen, but not much. Mamma has moved back to New York, so we have the place to ourselves. I'm also moving back there soon. I tell Eirik that I don't really live in Oslo any more. Eirik sits down on the edge of the bed. He laughs. He has bright blue eyes, long fair hair. I sit down next to him, take off my sweater and help him take off his. My skin's still peeling from the burn. Eirik pulls large flakes from under my breasts. It stings. I put my hand to his cheek where his wisdom teeth were.

Everything hurts, he says, and we laugh.

You're sitting on the windowsill. Summer comes, then autumn again. Like the girl in the fairy tale, you play with a golden apple.

I sit down beside you and look out.

You give me your apple. But it's not made of gold. It's an ordinary red apple. Red like the leaves on the ground. Red like K's jeep.

The girl I was and the woman I am both have a red woolly hat. It's not the same hat, I didn't keep the one I wore in 1983, but they're alike.

In any case, it's time to wrap up warm again, you say, it'll soon be November.

But first I want to sit here for a while, I say.

We'll sit here together, you say.

K uses his tongue. No one's done that before. I'm not very good at this. I come almost immediately. He does everything, I do nothing. I try not to breathe, he kisses, strokes, jabs, I want to make it last. Don't stop, I say. He lifts his head (stops) and laughs, almost gently, and a little bit surprised.

He spits on his fingers and makes me wetter than I am already. Do you know what we're going to do now, he says, turning me over on to my stomach.

His hands, his tongue, his dick, but then – it happens from one moment to the next – I don't want more. I had wanted it to last. It was me, my body, my greedy body saying yes. But then – no. He's not finished yet, is he? It's not that I don't want to any more. Or perhaps it is, perhaps that's exactly what it is. Desire gone. He's so much more experienced than I am. I don't know anything. I've been with boys before, *Eirik*, that's true, but now I'm here, swathed in K's white sheets like a big, motionless child.

A big, motionless child who's already let him know that what he was doing was good, every part of her arching towards him.
*Don't stop*, she'd said.
A big, motionless child who's not reciprocating.
What else?
Swathed in white sheets, holding him tight as can be.


But then, abruptly: I want to go home, she cries, I want to go to my hotel. The one whose name she can't remember.

I get up and go into the bathroom with the blue tiles. I kneel down at the toilet bowl and vomit. I don't know for how long I'm there. I haven't eaten all day. *No, that's not true.* Mia gave me some baguette in the apartment she shared with the translator girl, before we went on to the nightclub. Mia's name wasn't Mia. Z's name wasn't Z. I vomit again. K's name isn't K and he won't like it that I wrap myself in his big white expensive towels and lie down on the bathroom floor.

*Aren't you going to go back in?*

Yes, I will. Soon. I just need to lie here a moment and gather myself.


Come back here, won't you, K calls from the bed.

III

White

It's the middle of February 1983 when the telephone starts ringing in the shadowy apartment on the thirteenth floor. The sun shines into the empty rooms, on to the polished wood floors. The window ledges are white with snow. The Central Park treetops are white. The Columbus Avenue sidewalks are white. The city is still. The snow falls and falls, it's the worst snowstorm in thirty-six years, the TV news anchor says. The schools are closed. I'm at home. Abandoned vehicles litter the highways whose traffic can normally be heard to the west if you open the windows and listen; parked cars have to be dug out of the drifts. The papers can't be delivered on time, or else can't be delivered at all. New Yorkers must turn on their television sets or listen to the radio to stay informed. *There was an unearthly quiet over the city as winds whispered in the nearly deserted canyons of Manhattan*, the *New York Times* reported a few days later, *even Times Square had a feel of peace under a dazzling late-morning sun, its denizens out of sight.*

We have four telephones in the apartment and sometimes they all ring at once. We have one in the living room, one in the kitchen, one in Mamma's room and one in my room. The telephones are a faded brown, almost beige, no, almost white, each with a long cord that allows you to walk around, or lie on the sofa, or sit by the window, while still talking, and each has four buttons that light up according to which number has been called – the first line is the office number, the second is the home number, the third is my number and the fourth is Mamma's number. Her *secret* number.

Occasionally, though not very often, the fourth button will light up, and when it does Mamma runs into her room and shuts the door behind her.

The girl I was and the woman I am devour the press from the snow-filled days in February 1983. I'd been home from Paris a few weeks already. Did I think about what had happened? I can't remember that I did. With time, many events can be recast as something beautiful; give it a few hours, or days, or years. Memories of snow, for instance, like here in the *Times*: *The storm left scenes of wild beauty on city streets and suburban byways. Children climbed and tumbled on mountains of snow that had transformed familiar places into settings of wonder: the house suddenly had a different shape; cars and park benches became lumps, trees were graceful visions of black and white.*

No one's home but me. It's the middle of the day, around noon, quiet inside and out because of the snow. The radiator is turned up way too high and I pad barefoot from the kitchen, through the hall, to my room.

I picture her, the girl who once padded around in my body. She's got an army-green T-shirt on (*The Clash, Combat Rock* Tour) that just barely reaches over her thighs. Sometimes she wears it as a dress, and when she goes out she'll pair it with thick black tights, a shiny white belt around the waist, and black knee-high boots.

Hello?

She picks up the phone and sits down on the bed.

K says nothing, but right away she knows it's him, recognizes his laugh. It's not malicious by any means. He sounds happy to hear her voice.

You disappeared, he says.

I *left*.

You shouldn't have. We could have figured things out.

I don't know, I wanted to go home.

*I want to go home*, always the whiny child. But things don't have to end here, do they?

What do you mean?

I mean that I want to see you.

I don't know.

You can come over. I'm back in New York.

The girl looks out at the falling snow.

Well, I can't today.

Because of the storm, you mean?

I think it's weird they're calling it a storm. Closing the schools. Everything grinding to a halt. Back home we'd never call this a storm.

He laughs softly.

You're from Norway, right?

Yeah, but you know that.

So what's home for you, Norway or New York?

I don't know. New York, maybe.

She's about to expand on this – what's home. But then he cuts her off.

I miss you, he says. I want to see you. I want you to come over. Don't say no.

He goes quiet.

Okay, the girl says, lying down under the blanket, the phone pressed to her ear, I won't say no.

She sees before her the white towels hanging from their pegs in the bathroom in the Paris apartment, how she wrapped herself up in them, first one, then another, then a third, as if the towels were bandages, and how she lay on that cold blue-tiled floor so silently and without moving.

I'll call you again tomorrow, he says. Maybe the storm will've gone by then.

He laughs, then corrects himself.

Maybe the thing that *isn't* a storm will be over, and then all you have to do is put on the leather jacket you wore the first time I saw you in the elevator, hop on a bus, and get your beautiful little ass over here.

One morning, three months and a thousand years after you appeared under an elm tree in the park, I lay down on my bathroom floor with no real plan to get up again. After assessing what I'd begun to refer to as *the situation* (the floating, the soaring, the terror, the trembling), and with lots of help from you, I concluded that I was no longer capable of taking a shower. Among other things. I mean, I knew *how* it was done. I had gone through (and continued going through as I lay on the floor) the necessary steps: *take off bathrobe, step into shower, turn on water, lather body with soap, rinse body, turn off water, step out of shower, dry body with white towel from peg on far left.* But it was impossible. The list was never-ending. Or lists. There was never just one. Because after the shower – then what? It goes on and on. Indefinitely. I haven't answered emails or text messages for weeks, months. My friends are giving up on me. I talk too loudly and too much, or not at all. And when I *do* speak – it's not my voice. I'm deceiving everyone. I'm more you than me now.

 I say that I *lay down* on the bathroom floor, but that's not exactly true, I was still (after the incident on Vogts Street) *floating* or *soaring*, only a few millimetres up, yes, it was barely noticeable, but enough for me not to feel the ground beneath my feet, or the floor under my body. Still, at this moment in time I was so worn out – hollowed out is perhaps a more precise way of putting it – that I didn't care whether the right words were *worn out* or *hollowed out*; *lying*, *floating* or *soaring*. I looked for my phone, found it in my bathrobe pocket and searched for an analyst who might be able to fit me in for a same-day appointment. Preferably within the hour. Impatience was a surprising aspect of this terror. The more listless I became, the more impatient too. It was *physical* – the listlessness combined with the impatience – the itching under the skin of my face, the twitching of my legs, the panic.

I found two.

Two analysts, both women.

I looked at the photos they had chosen for their websites; first one, then the other.

Was it the same with analysts as with hairdressers – that if they could fit you in on that day they probably weren't very good? I studied their faces – their faces would decide which one I chose. And maybe their names. One was called Maria, the other Martha, like the sisters in the Gospel of Luke, Mary and Martha, and of the two I've always liked Martha the best.

Martha, Martha.

Dark eyes, a warm gaze. A good face.

I entered my details and booked a session. *Can you help me?* I got up off the floor (managed that okay), counted my steps back to the bedroom, dug out a pair of sweatpants and a threadbare jumper from my wardrobe. I can't remember how I got there. I don't drive, so I must have taken the bus, or maybe my husband gave me a lift.

And then there we were, face to face, Martha and I.

I think I'm going to die, I said.

What makes you think that?

I'm very afraid.

Well, we're all going to die eventually, said Martha.

And of course she was right about that, but she hadn't the calm look in her eyes that she had in her photo. Her face was different in real life. She looked worried, or sad, or lonely, I don't know.

Something was off. She asked about my childhood. I told her a story. She livened up, not much, but enough to now look fairly interested, and so I livened up too, words pouring from my lips.

These are all things we can talk about, she said after a while.

What things? I said.
Your relationship with your mother, your father. Your childhood.

When the session came to an end, we agreed on a new appointment. I thanked her profusely, repeating over and over what a great help she'd been. On my way to the bus stop I cancelled it.

From the bathroom floor.
Two of the most beautiful lines in Jane Kenyon's poem about melancholy — I struggle to translate them, to find the right words in Norwegian.

> *You taught me to exist without gratitude*
> *You ruined my manners toward God.*

The first is fairly straightforward:
*Du lærte meg å eksistere uten takknemlighet*
But then — the one about God, that's where things go awry:
*Du ødela min gode oppførsel overfor Gud.*
Not good enough.
*ruined*
*manners*
*toward*
It won't do.

I take my phone out of my bathrobe pocket and send my husband a text.

*Can you translate* You ruined my manners towards God? *Or is it untranslatable?*


I'll lie here until someone decides to come home.

January 2020.

*The lies you make me tell —*
    I'm writing a new book
    I get up early, shower and get dressed
    I'm afraid I'm quite busy and will have to take a raincheck
    I didn't see your email
    I'm sorry, I can't hear a thing you're saying

I *can* hear it, or at least the part of my brain that's still working can. It can *hear* how laughable they are, the lies and fears you keep lugging about, like a cat with a half-eaten bird between its teeth, *What's the matter with you,* say the walls and the floor and the ceiling, *pull yourself together.*
    *And where do you get —*
    that red is a poisonous colour
    that you're floating and soaring

that there's something wrong with your inner ear
that you want to live but don't know how


All this as well as the fear of the fear growing exponentially every single day.

But you love (your children, your grandchild, your husband, your big brother, your sisters, your mother, your friends, and innumerable pieces that have saved your life . . . written, composed, painted, woven, photographed, choreographed, played, danced . . . you love the park outside your window with its deciduous trees that you count, one, two, three, four, five; you love the ghosts, ten, maybe more; you love your dog . . . and many of these souls . . . the works . . . the trees . . . can bear witness to suffering you haven't even begun to fathom) and still you're incapable of pulling yourself together.

February 2020.

You walked beside me, wrapped yourself around me, wound yourself within me; we shared lungs, a voice, a brain, a face; we were half me, half you. I can't say for certain if the planned Teuva trip was your scheme or mine. A scheme, though, it was. First I booked a flight to Helsinki, then I went online and worked out a route: train from Helsinki to Seinäjoki, bus from Seinäjoki to Teuva. I was stirred by the foreign place names. It had been a long time since I'd been stirred by anything. I searched the Internet again. Teuva (population somewhere between five thousand and six thousand, depending on your source) is a mainly Finnish-speaking municipality bordering on those of Karijoki, Kauhajoki, Kristiinankaupunki, Kurikka and Närpiö.

In the summer of 1953, Tove Jansson (herself a world traveller) painted a five-metre-wide altarpiece mural in Teuva Church in South Ostrobothnia. I can't stop thinking about it. It depicts the ten virgins from the parable in the Gospel of Matthew, their lit and unlit lamps, the magnificent bridegroom.

*

Five are wise and five are foolish – or *bad* as some of the Norwegian translations of the Gospels would have it. Foolish, bad, unprepared. They are late for the wedding banquet and cry out: *Lord, Lord, open for us!* And are met by the irrevocable words: *Verily I say unto you, I know you not.*

Ten willowy girls in long robes, white, grey, blue, lilac. The wise ones have halos about their heads, the foolish ones have not. A piece of red cloth lies on the ground – a pool of blood, or an exquisite length of silk? I don't know if the splotch of red is meant to signal danger or hope. Perhaps both – the wise virgins' lamps are aglow, the approaching bridegroom luminous.

I find the altarpiece online while writing about the sixteen-year-old girl's brief exchanges a long time ago with the fever-sick Professor Claus on a flight bound for Paris. Jansson's depiction of the five wise and five foolish virgins is beautiful, almost serene, despite the apocalyptic theme of the parable it's meant to interpret. One of the white-clad virgins stands next to the bridegroom, who seems as if just moments ago – and to his astonishment – he stepped into the picture from the wall on which it is painted. I notice the white-clad virgin because of her slightly bowed head, like she's bestowing a kiss. Is she kissing her well-lit lamp (she's one of the wise ones) or, perhaps, the lips of a girl? But there's no such girl. Or, if there is, she's not supposed to be there; she's nearly invisible, like a ghost, like the painting's secret, in the perpetual state of either disappearing or coming into being. I think of you and me and look once more at the mural. The white-clad virgin presses her wise and lovely mouth to the invisible girl's lips and draws the girl towards her, into the glow of her halo. Tove Jansson has placed this embrace (which perhaps exists only in my imagination) in front of an angular rock, a rock that could equally be the lower part of the girl's robe. The more I look at it, look at her, the more distinct she becomes, like an eleventh virgin, and this is why I make arrangements to go to Teuva: to see if she, to see if you exist.


I once planned a trip to New Mexico just so I could see Georgia O'Keeffe's rust-red mountainsides. O'Keeffe's landscapes have always reminded me of my father. When my father died he fell silent, which, of course, was to be expected, but I kept looking for ways to revoke that silence. I never did go to New Mexico. And I never went to Teuva either. In March 2020 the world shut down. The church in Teuva started streaming its services to empty pews. I logged on a few times and followed the proceedings online. The minister spoke in Finnish and I didn't understand a word, but now and then I caught a glimpse of the altarpiece in the background, behind the pulpit.

And K kept calling on the telephone that winter after we'd both returned from Paris.

When are you coming?
   stop by after school
      I think about you all the time


As I'm writing this, it occurs to me that now I'm the one thinking about him. *All the time.* It's not an exaggeration, like when he said it. I really do think about him. Except he doesn't know. He doesn't know that there's a woman in Oslo, in the Torshov area, walking her dog in the park (underneath the elm trees, in between the lamp posts) who's giving him all her attention. He doesn't remember her name, her skin, her hands. I can't be sure, but he probably doesn't remember. He doesn't realize that after all these years he is once again standing – sitting – lying – naked in front of her, being looked at.

    She sees him waking up, falling asleep, smiling, crying out as he comes (he closed his eyes, I kept mine wide open), sees him again now, many years later, sees him old, maybe frail, maybe poor in health, in his eighties, not long left.

One winter night in 1983 a girl lost her way. To find her – and this was the original undertaking – I had to find him too. I had to find them together, not leave them in peace. Why? Because the girl won't leave *me* in peace. *Look at me*, she says from the blue-tiled bathroom floor with just a white towel around her.

*You, you, you.* Not even our mother knows there are two of us. You came in autumn, waited for me in the park, wrapped yourself around me, a single stem at first, then another, then another, and soon your tendrils reached into me with an urgency that was relentless, climbing upwards, extending downwards and out to the sides, your vines grew very strong, until one day there was more of you than me, green in spring, red, yellow and brown in autumn, beautiful and perilous.


He exists – K exists – his dark curly hair – his hands – his tongue – the words he said to me – *neurotic little bitch* – everything exists in the alphabet I have made for us all these years later.

The snowstorm has subsided in New York, but hundreds of fires sweep across southern Australia. High summer temperatures, strong winds and the absence of rain has a disastrous impact on the eucalyptus forests of Victoria. The PLO finds President Reagan's Middle East peace plan unacceptable. It's 23 February 1983. The *Times* carries an article about a new American telescope having revealed cosmic 'maternity wards' where clouds of interstellar gas and dust appear to be in various stages of giving birth to stars. I get up, shower, wash and dry my hair, tie it in a high ponytail, put on a long white men's shirt with a black leather belt around my waist, thick black tights, the oversized leather jacket (the one he asked me to wear) and black knee-high boots. First, I'm going to school. I've been absent for weeks. I don't know what to expect. Will Monsieur O roll his eyes at me? The teachers keep sending letters to my mother that I intercept and return with her signature. She never sees them. I taught myself to sign her name when I was little and still living in Oslo. After school I'll walk a few blocks north and a few blocks east to the building where K lives and works.

We have a date. He said he'd be waiting for me.

The email subject line announces: *Lose the ability to lose things*, which sounds frightening. Every day I get emails from companies trying to sell me stuff. I don't want emails. I don't want to lose the ability to lose things. I want every company, every domain that's ever approached me, to lose all the contacts they have, especially mine. It doesn't matter how many times I click Unsubscribe, it doesn't work. Every day (or almost every day – *stop exaggerating! Be precise!*) my inbox is full of these emails. This time they want me to buy a device that makes it easier to find the things you tend to lose – keys, glasses, etc. With the help of this device – and an app on your phone – you'll be able to find your things right away, without ever actually having to look for them. Provided (it occurs to me) you haven't already lost your phone. The idea is to make *looking for things* an obsolete activity.

My mind, for instance. I've lost it. Or not *it* exactly. But many features associated with it that I used to delight in, like my sanity, my manners, my deportment, my good sense. Ever since you appeared under an elm tree in September almost two years ago, I've looked for ways to lose *you*, but to no avail.

*

When you returned after all those years of having been gone, it felt like falling in love – except the wrong way round. You took up vast amounts of space. You demanded my undivided attention. You wrapped yourself around me and swore you'd never leave.

You resembled neither a memory nor a story.

I gave myself to you.

In his short story 'Funes the Memorious', Jorge Luis Borges presents a young man, Ireneo Funes, who – after having been thrown by a half-tamed horse – sustains a brain injury that results in him remembering everything he's ever experienced. It's a terrible thing. Much worse than anything I've known, because I am a forgetter and a writer. I can resort to imagination and desire.

Not so for the main character in the Borges piece. After being thrown by the horse, Ireneo Funes loses his ability to forget – to forget anything he's ever seen, heard, dreamed, read and known. Borges writes about the *wary light of dawn* falling on Ireneo Funes's face as the narrator finally catches a glimpse of it. Ireneo Funes is a young man, only nineteen years old, but perceived *as monumental as bronze, more ancient than Egypt, older than the prophecies and the pyramids*. Borges recounts in detail – Funes's memory-drenched world teems with details – the terror of perfect memory, without a single opportunity to seek shelter (or light) in the language of imagination and oblivion.

*

Again, this notion of causality that I'm not sure I even believe in but reluctantly go along with. Is there always a reason? *Thrown by a horse.* Or can a person's anguish be passed on from one generation to the next? When my father died, I inherited a black-and-white poster of the dancer and choreographer Pina Bausch. Maybe I also inherited his depressions, anxiety and rage? In that case, I may be struggling to get rid of, to get to the bottom of, or to lose, what isn't even mine but my father's, or his father's, or his father's.

In the spring of 1965, a year and a half before I was born, my father admitted himself to the psychiatric ward of Stockholm's Sophiahemmet Hospital.

He was so afraid of losing – losing his mind, losing his prowess, losing his good health, losing his desire, losing his language, losing his strength, losing control, losing the line he'd so carefully plotted from one point to another and another. Everything he'd prepared so meticulously, down to the smallest detail.

In his diary entry for 29 April 1965, he writes:

*I shall try to keep to the following guidelines. If possible.*
*– Breakfast at seven thirty with the other patients.*
*– Immediately thereafter, morning routines and a walk.*

— *No newspapers or magazines during writing hours.*
— *No contact whatsoever with the theatre.*
— *Receive no letters, telegrams or telephone messages.*
— *Visits home permitted in the evenings.*
— *Certain trips to the movies and some TV allowed.*
*I feel that the final battle is fast approaching and everything now rests on my ability to stop procrastinating and to get back to work.*


My father always told me to write things down or else I'd lose – forget – what was important. Years ago, right after my first husband and I divorced, my son Ola and I moved into an apartment at Majorstua in Oslo. Ola was six, I was twenty-nine. I remember trying to cram as many packing boxes as I could into the storage space in the attic. It was then, at the time of the divorce and the move, that I caught a glimpse of the white wire-bound notebook with nothing written in it, just a photograph tucked between its pages – it was the photo K took of me in Paris.

I kept a diary at the time, page after page mostly about everyday things:

Books I'd read (Marlen Haushofer's *The Wall*, Ingeborg Bachmann's *The Thirtieth Year*. I remember at the time being startled and frequently overwhelmed – I too was in my thirtieth year – by what Bachmann calls *harsh rays of light*).

Notes for a novel I was working on. *Two sisters, one survives, the other doesn't.*

Quotes from books I liked. Words hastily jotted down. Lists of words. Norwegian and English. Definitions copied from dictionaries and encyclopedias.

I can't find anything in my diary (from when I was a young divorcee and single mother) about the photograph K took of me, nothing about discovering it in the attic, in between the blank pages of a white wire-bound notebook, nothing to suggest that I – or the twenty-nine-year-old version of me – thought very much about the series of events that took place in Paris some years earlier, in the winter of 1983.

From my diary 1996/2020.

'A saline lake'
Depression

Latin *dēpressiōn-em*, noun of action < *dēprimĕre* to press down, depress: perhaps immediately

*Pathology:* Lowering of the vital functions or powers; a state of reduced vitality
*Economy:* A long-lasting period of greatly reduced general economic activity
*Music:* Lowering in pitch, flattening (of the voice, or a musical note)
*Surgery:* The operation of couching for cataracts
*Meteorology:* A centre of minimum pressure, or the system of winds around it
*Astronomy:* The angular distance of a star, the pole, etc., below the horizon
*Gunnery:* The lowering of the muzzle of a gun below the horizontal line
*Psychology:* Frequently a sign of psychiatric disorder or a component of various psychoses,

with symptoms of misery, anguish or guilt accompanied by headache, insomnia, etc.

*Geology*: Part of the earth's surface lying below sea level – e.g. 'at the bottom of the depression is a saline lake'

I haven't held on to many things from when I was sixteen. I've kept a diary for most of my life – but not of that year. Or the year after. I have a few photographs, a few letters, but nothing that can shed light on what I'm writing about here. For a long time I hoped I'd discover something, an almanac perhaps, a letter, a note, that would jog my memory: *Ah, yes, now I remember!* I've pictured my forgetfulness as a large piece of cloth, a shroud perhaps, or a woven tapestry – blue, red, white and maybe a splash of green. I convinced myself that if only I was attentive enough, vigilant enough, I'd figure out how to do away with the cloth, draw it to one side, unhook it, roll it up: *Of course! That's how it was.* But the girl from 1983 wraps herself in all kinds of fabric, and won't let me near. One evening the dog and I were out walking in the park, round and round we went, and I kept thinking about the photographs in my high-school senior yearbook from 1984. I'd been leafing through its pages, looking at pictures all afternoon, and still I had no memory of Monsieur O – the French teacher. It didn't matter how many times I looked at his face. *Nothing*. I looked at my own yearbook photo as well. So this is her, the soon-to-be-high-school-graduate: a heavily made-up seventeen-year-old, a slip of a girl, in a black turtleneck and black jeans.

After Paris – there are gleams of light here and there, like scattered stars in a winter sky, the rest is forgotten. There is no story. I draw a line from one star to another to another, and so on, imagining a pattern in the shape of a ring, or like the Winter Hexagon. It's not the same as remembering, but similar. Whenever you get lost, hiking in the mountains, for instance, or walking around in a strange city, chances are you've been going in circles. You thought you were moving forward in a straight line, but eventually you stumble upon your own footprints and realize you're right back where you started. It's like writing.

What I remember is –

K calling me again and again after I came back from Paris. I remember Claude. I remember that my first boyfriend, the one I've given the name Eirik, came to visit me in New York. Eirik was my first. He was eighteen and I was fifteen. The day after we slept together, I lay in the sun all day, sometimes falling asleep, and ended up with blistering second-degree burns. The scars on my chest appear and fade and then appear again; sometimes, when they're at their most visible, reminding me of a big red bird's footprints.

*

Eirik stayed at a small run-down Upper West Side hotel. We'd been writing to each other for some time, ever since I left Oslo. The letters are lost. I remember asking myself, while we were writing and especially as his visit to New York approached, whether we were still boyfriend-girlfriend?

In February 1983, not long after Maxine witnessed something she wasn't meant to witness, she told me there wasn't much she or anyone else could do for me now. I was done. No photographer wanted to hire me. I was the girl who'd left Paris for no good reason. I was the girl who made bad choices. Maxine didn't say in so many words that I was to blame for my new-found unhireable status, but I gathered that I was and that I should be ashamed of myself. Because clearly, my dear, this has to do with a sense of shame. Or shamelessness. I mean, have you *no* shame? After that, I started going to clubs and staying out late.

When Eirik came to visit – nineteen, gangly, long blond hair – I took him out with me. I drank more than him, danced more than him, talked more than him.

He said: You've changed.

Well, of course I have.

No, I mean your face, he said.

His English wasn't very good, and even though he asked me to, I never translated what other people were saying. He was jet-lagged. I remember that. Disoriented and lost in a strange city. I said, *Come on, don't be a wuss.* It was already May. Eirik's father had told him to go and see the cherry blossom trees in Central Park. I said we would, but we didn't.

One night that May, Eirik and I went for a drive with a man I'd known for a year or so. The man isn't important. I remember him, but that is coincidental. I could just as well have forgotten. The man and I had made a date to meet at a club downtown so I could give him back the leather jacket I had borrowed from him several months before. The man, an acquaintance more than a friend, was a lot older than me, a lot older than Eirik, but younger than K. Eirik was in the back seat. The man said – actually, I don't remember what he said – but words to the effect of: *Let's drop the kid off and go have a drink at my place.* I remember laughing and nodding and Eirik saying something in Norwegian. I didn't turn around and ask him what it was. We drove up Tenth Avenue. I cranked up the volume on the radio. 'Let's Dance' blared out through the open windows. I waved my arms in time to the beat.

I caught Bowie live in Toronto just a few weeks ago, the man said, and stepped on the gas.

I lit a cigarette and laughed. And then he – the man – said he didn't really need his leather jacket back after all. Eirik's voice again. *Can you turn around and look at me?* There was a red light. As we waited for green the man leaned over and kissed me. His mouth was wet and slobbering and smelled of gin. Eirik went quiet. The leather jacket cracked and squeaked as I let myself be kissed again.


The years 1982 to 1984 unfold like a long white winter in my mind's eye, though with the occasional strain of other seasons, other colours. Eirik went back to Norway a week or so earlier than planned.

I'm going home, he said.

Yeah, well, you know, I replied, and then there wasn't much else to say.


Months later, in the autumn of 1983, I saw K on the corner of 57th and Seventh. He was leaning against the wall of a building talking to a tall, dark-haired woman. It was windy out, and people had come from all over the world to see the autumn foliage in Central Park. I drew the leather jacket tighter around me. *If he turns around and looks across the street, he'll see me.* K put his arm around the tall woman and they walked along Seventh Avenue, before disappearing into a restaurant a few blocks further down.

There was student I'll call John. We went to the same high school for a while, but he's not pictured in the yearbook. I leaf through its pages, looking specifically for this boy, but there's no trace of him. I talked to him only once, in the cafeteria. By then more than a year had passed since I came back from Paris, more than a year since K called on the telephone asking me to come over, more than a year since I ran into Claude one last time at K's studio, and exactly a year since Eirik came to New York and left abruptly a few days later.

The spring semester of 1984 was my last before starting university. Whenever I went to school, a little bit more often this year than the year before, everyone was always talking about John, who seemed to have disappeared so suddenly from the face of the earth. Talked about him in the hallway, talked about him in the classroom, before the teacher arrived. Hushed voices, a constant murmur. I remember thick, dark strands of hair falling into his eyes, his long, lean dancer arms, his upright, elegant posture. I remember that time in the cafeteria, before he was gone, when he carefully rolled out a poster he'd just bought at a dancewear store near Lincoln Center. He couldn't wait to show me. Show *someone* — I just happened to be there.

Be careful, he said, we mustn't spill anything on it! He laid the poster, now unfurled, on the table.

It was late afternoon, the cafeteria had emptied and was about to close. We'd bought blueberry muffins and black coffee, and he was determined to protect his newly purchased treasure from greasy fingermarks and coffee stains.

The poster showed the dancer Judith Jamison, white-clad, performing *Cry*, choreographed for her some years earlier by Alvin Ailey. Not many can pull it off, John said, because this piece is one of the hardest things the female body can perform. I saw her onstage, he continued, and couldn't breathe afterwards. Have you ever, he asked, have you ever experienced ...? And then he went quiet, looking at the poster, gesturing for me to look at it too and to never take my eyes off it. Judith Jamison is the reason I came to New York and became a dancer, he declared after a little while. All I have to do is close my eyes and imagine her in her white ruffled dress to evoke her courage ... *courage* is the right word ... the courage of her movements. And then, after a pause: So even though *Cry* is a work dedicated to the plight of women, I always thought, growing up in Philadelphia, that it spoke directly to me, even though, you know, I'm a guy.

\*

The reason I remember this scene in the school cafeteria is that the exact same poster — the one of Judith Jamison — hangs on the wall in the narrow hall of the apartment I share with my husband, our daughter Eva and the old dog. It hangs opposite another poster, left to me by my father, of Pina Bausch — she too entirely in white.

Judith Jamison saved my life, John said, I mean, when I was a kid.
We're still just kids, I said.
What world are you living in? he said. You're seventeen, right? I'm sixteen. We haven't been kids since we were twelve.
But how did she save your life?
She's so fucking alive, so full of possibility, I look at her and *I'm* possible too.
And then he asked me where I felt most at home, in Oslo or New York.
I'm not sure, I said.
What language do you dream in?
I'm not really sure about that either.
The language you dream in is where you belong, he posited.
He rummaged in his duffel bag, took out his warm-up pants and placed them on the table, then his jock, his ballet shoes, his leotard, his tights, his socks, his resistance bands, his water bottle, foot roller, massage ball,

can of hairspray and finally his sweatshirt, all of which he laid out on the table, before finally finding what he was looking for: another picture (this one silver-framed), of a big white dog.

He's bigger than the apartment I live in here, he said. You can't have a dog in New York. At least not this one.

We stood for a moment in silence considering the dog in the photograph.

My dog's as big as a tree, he said, and gestured to suggest trees, a forest of white birch.

And then he was gone. Perhaps that's why I remember him. Not because of the poster, but because he went missing. First everyone blamed it on the kissing disease. March–April–May 1984. Mono was the reason he didn't come back to school. Then it was pneumonia. And then someone suggested that he'd probably gone back to Philadelphia. As May became June, I overheard the school librarian (the same librarian who three years earlier had found the books and magazines featuring pictures of Twiggy) say to one of the teachers that John had AIDS. So now it begins, she said, her voice almost inaudible, and it never ends.

I've borrowed Mamma's summer house to write. On the crammed pine bookshelves in the living room, I happen upon a copy of *A Tale of Two Cities* with what looks like a pencil drawing of a shivering, emaciated prisoner on the cover. Mamma has written inside the book, little notes in the margins, exclamation marks and scribbles. With a fine black felt-tip she has underlined the sentence: *I have heard whispers from old voices.*

Everything is pine. The bookcase, the floor, the ceiling. On little nails knocked into the walls (also pine) hang the framed black-and-white photographs of mostly dead relatives, women in buttoned-up dresses, men in uniform, and among them a picture of Mamma when she was a little girl.

The picture is from just after the war. She's around nine years old, standing close to her mother. Her mother (Nanna) is in the middle, flanked by Mamma on the one side and Mamma's sister, the elder of the two girls, on the other.

Nanna is still a young woman in the photograph, around thirty-five.

I remove the picture from the frame to see if there's anything written on the back. I find neither the name of the photographer nor the year in which the picture was taken, but my guess would be 1947 or 1948. I'm at a loss and a little startled when confronted with the smiles of Nanna, then a young woman, and her two little girls, because I can't perceive them as anything other than strangely forced, disfigured by reserve and purported happiness – or not exactly happiness, but certainly a gesture for everyone to see, a sign, a manifestation, a salutation, a cry, a declaration to the effect that all is well. The war is over. Father is dead. The economy is broken. Nanna is ill, and will soon be diagnosed with tuberculosis and admitted to Ringvål Sanitorium. But we won't have any of that in the picture. Forget about the things that hurt us. Let bygones be bygones and come what may. All shall be well and all shall be well and all shall be well.

I place a hand over my mother's sister's face to see if I can detect a special intimacy between Mamma and Nanna – mother and daughter – and once the older sister is gone from view, I see a girl nestling against her mother's body as if she can't ever get close enough. There's a hint of trepidation in her smile that I can't detect in the other two. I look at all three again. Two girls and a woman photographed from the waist up. The woman (Nanna) is cute, but not exceptional in any way, a bit anonymous, perhaps, in a floral-patterned V-necked dress, a simple string of pearls around her neck.


A young widow and her two little girls are having their photograph taken. It's 1947 or 1948. The three of them do exactly as instructed by the photographer, smile, don't blink. When the image is framed and hung on the wall of their tiny two-room apartment in Trondheim, visitors will say that it's a lovely picture. All three are wearing their hair in the short, wavy bob that was fashionable at the time; Mamma and her sister in their Sunday best, ironed blouses and identical apron dresses. Mamma's blouse, white with a fastening at the neck, is probably a hand-me-down and plainer than her older sister's blouse with its embroidered flowers on the collar.


The dog and I are walking past the green cornfields, I have my mother on the phone. I can hear her breathing.
    It's marvellous, she says.
    What is?
    That you can look up dead people on the internet and find out what happened to them.


The next day the dog is sprawled out on the floor. I'm sitting at the large old pinewood table, working.
    Mamma calls. She asks me to look up a name that

came to her while she was half asleep. I may just have dreamed it, she says.

I abandon the text I'm working on and type the name into the search bar. I tell her the half-dreamed name is real. Or was.

He's dead now, I say. He died in the 1970s.

His name was Helge Sol, which is to say it was another name entirely, but that's what I'm calling him here. Chief physician Helge Sol, tall, pale, pinched, a respected former resident of the city of Trondheim.

I find an old black-and-white photograph of him and send it to Mamma using the complicated system we've devised involving email and fax.

Are we allowed not to forgive the dead? she asks with photograph in hand.

I don't know, I say. I think so.

The image on the fax is blurry – ghostlike – but she recognizes the face right away.

Yes, she cries, it's him!

I picture her in the creaky, labyrinthine house in Gloucester, alone in the kitchen, sitting on a spindle-back chair, looking at the red maple tree outside her window. She can hear it, it's always there, the rustling, the wind, the leaves. She looks at the tree, she looks at the blurry fax-photo in front of her on the table.

Once, Mamma was a little girl of nine or ten years old, too scared to go to school. Now and then she'd take to her bed, telling her mother she was sick. A headache. A tummy ache. A hot cloth on her brow. *Mamma, I think I have a fever.* Her mother (Nanna: snappy dresses, short grey hair) went along with the stories, *my poor little darling*, she said, stroking her daughter's hair. But then one day – no more going along with any of it. One day she rang for the doctor, the tall, pale, pinched doctor Helge Sol, whom she knew only slightly, or perhaps a little more than *only slightly*, and asked him to please come to the apartment and then, when he presented himself a little later, she led him directly into the bedroom Mamma shared with her sister.

Good day, said the doctor.

Good day, said Mamma.

And then he said: So we're feeling ill, are we?

Yes, Mamma said, and pulled the cover up to her chin, hiding her scrawny little ribcage from the doctor's gaze.

Some days were better than others and on a good day Mamma could play her ribcage as if her ribs were the strings of a banjo while at the same time whistling *Oh, Susanna, don't you cry for me*, and she could recite the whole of 'The Little Match Girl' and make everyone listening burst into tears, she could hurtle down the streets of the town on her red bicycle, one foot on the saddle, one foot in the air, but on this particular day, a winter's day in 1948, let's say, she's in bed, hiding under the covers. Imploringly, she looks at her mother as Helge Sol orders her to get up and get dressed. Imploringly, yes, but her mother looks away. The doctor, on the other hand, won't take his eyes off her: she gets up out of bed, takes off her white nightdress and stands naked, barefoot on the cold wooden floor; all this while he takes her in, twenty-four ribs, breasts no bigger than bumblebee stings. She crosses the floor, finds her dress in the wardrobe and, finally, goes with him to the hospital, where Dr Helge Sol orders her admission to the ward for *seriously ill children*, as a punishment, she tells me, because I lied, I said I was sick and couldn't go to school.

Mamma tells me about her sister – she with the embroidered flowers on her collar.

We slept in bunk beds, she begins, I had the top, she had the bottom. And long before my sister started going out at night, long before my mother was diagnosed with tuberculosis and admitted to Ringvål Sanatorium, long before she came home from Ringvål Sanatorium and started going out at night too, long before I was left alone lying in the top bunk in the empty apartment in the building known as Forsikringsgården, afraid of the dark, afraid of being alone, *scared, scared, scared*, long before I was admitted to the ward for seriously ill children as punishment for having lied, long before any of this, my sister and I would sing to each other every night before going to sleep.

Mamma sings gently –

> *Safe we are from all our fears,*
> *God's children to His heart so dear;*
> *The timid bird that hideth must,*
> *The star so high above the dust.*

The hymn has six verses, Mamma tells me, but every time we got to the fourth verse we always started laughing, we just couldn't help imagining God counting every hair on every head of every child in the whole world, how many did he get to, and how long did it take before he could start counting all the tears, and after a while the only verse we ever sang was the fourth one.

> *Each hair He counts upon our head,*
> *And every tear that we must shed;*
> *He feeds and clothes us, every one,*
> *And soothes our sorrows till they're gone.*

And once too I was the little girl lying next to Mamma in Mamma's bed.

It's a long time since 1948.

And 1983 is still a long way off. Eight, nine, ten, perhaps eleven years in the future. It's evening, soon night-time.

Mamma sings gently –

*Each hair He counts upon our head,*
*And every tear that we must shed;*
*He feeds and clothes us, every one,*
*And soothes our sorrows till they're gone.*

Mamma runs her hand through my hair.
    Now it's just you and me left in the whole wide world, she says.


Mamma's and my story is so steeped in love and forgetfulness that I have to reinvent us every day.

Paris, January 1983. I'm perching on a high chair getting my make-up done. A girl appears in the doorway. She's about to step into the big, bright, bunker-like studio, wearing a hat and coat. I have neither hat nor coat. I've been in Paris for more than twenty-four hours and the hat (red) and the coat (blue) lie folded on a chair in K's empty apartment where the lamps have been turned off, the big dishevelled room (the small table, stereo, liquor cabinet, bookshelves, the unmade bed with the white sheets) illuminated by winter light falling through the window.

The girl in the doorway is my age, perhaps even a year younger.

When you're sixteen, as I was then, you'd never *not* try to figure out how old someone is when you met them, especially if they're around your own age.

So – were you born in sixty-six, sixty-seven or sixty-five?

If you were born in the seventies, you're too young to matter.

The girl barely crosses the threshold before Claude starts screaming at her. Oh, for Chrissake! Stop right there! *What the fuck!*

I had no idea that nearly forty years on I'd still be able to hear Claude's voice in my head, slick and sly, not unlike the slickness of his coiffed hair.

*Vite, vite, vite*
*Stop right there*
*What the fuck*
*She's a piece of sex*

No, I hardly even notice Claude, the fat little man with expensive watches in his grubby overcoat, as I perch on the high chair in front of the mirror, beneath the glaring lights, about to have my make-up done by a guy of about twenty who, having picked out a fluffy brush, now dabs it into a small pot and sets about my face.

First a blank canvas, he says, and then the transformation.

*How old are you? Just turned sixteen? You look younger.*

He says: The point is to look like a twenty-year-old who looks like a fourteen-year-old.

I wish we could be friends. Can I tell him that? The make-up artist? If we were friends, we could go out, go to a café, go sit on a bench in the park and watch people pass by, invent stories about them.

They're creating their own beautiful little world here, he says, voice barely audible, where cradle-snatching is perfectly fine. He turns, casts a glance in the direction of K and Claude, all of them, assistants and editors milling about in the bunker. They're not the same assistants and editors as the day before, but act the same way. Busy. Important.

He blends colours on a palette, and when loud music spills out into the room he starts singing along, looking at us both in the mirror.

Do you like this one? he cries.

I nod, singing softly, *Here comes the* . . .

No, no, don't move, he says with a laugh, don't sing, don't move your lips or I won't be able to do your face.

Sorry, I say, and close my mouth. He can sing though.

*Here comes the mirror man*
*Says he's a people fan*


Yesterday can't compare with today. Yesterday I sat tucked away in a corner with a paper plate piled up with food I couldn't manage to eat. Yesterday I was in everyone's way.

Did I see you here yesterday? the young make-up artist asks. He leans forward, furrows his brow and examines my eyes in the mirror.

I shrug.

Yeah, I was here, I tell him, but I didn't stay very long.


I don't say anything about the day before – about coming here with Claude, about being tucked away in a corner and yet being in everyone's way, about being hungry and not eating and getting drunk on gin and tonic and walking up and down the streets with a scrap of paper in my hand, about trying to find my hotel so I could call Mamma and tell her that everything was fine, everything was fine. I don't tell him about yesterday, or about today for that matter, about this morning at around two thirty when I walked up the pitch-dark stairwell to K's apartment.

Because yesterday can't compare with today.

Today I've been in Paris for more than twenty-four hours. Today K will take my picture.

Today I woke up next to K, swathed in K's white sheets, nauseous and still jet-lagged and hurting all over.

*But not lost like you were yesterday?* someone asked, perhaps it was you.

No, not lost.

*And what exactly did you do when you woke up next to K?*

What did I do?

I sat up on my knees and wound the top sheet around my body. K lay sleeping with his mouth open, a dribble of saliva on his chin, breathing heavily. I leaned over and looked at his sleeping face. The winter sun fell in through the window, spilling a few drops of light on him. His dark curls were lustreless against the white pillow, his open mouth slack, his nose unimpressive, puny, and specked with little red blemishes I hadn't noticed before. All of him outstretched there before my eyes, naked under the covers. I lifted the blanket, looked at his body, up and down. His skinny, hairy legs, his soft cock, like a snail without a shell, his flabby belly now protruding, his wrinkled neck.

Can I just sit here in silence and look at him?

*Of course you can.*

I giggle softly.

What an ugly man he is, sleeping in his bed, oblivious, ignorant of being looked at, so old, so decrepit, so all out of tricks.

I don't know how long I sat there studying the details of his body arrested in sleep, but then, after a while, it seemed as if one more winter's day decided to commence, the sun flared in the sky and flooded the small Parisian apartment with light. K opened his eyes and looked straight up into mine.

*Fuck*, he said.

He looked scared. Or angry. Or both.

I shouldn't have looked at him while he was sleeping.

*Yes you should, why shouldn't you?*

He closed his eyes and opened them again, ran a hand through his hair, shook himself and sat up, pulling the sheet around him.

Now both of us were on our knees, face to face, wrapped in white sheets.

Good morning, he said, and grinned, the fear, the anger no longer quite so conspicuous. He stroked my cheek. He leaned back and glanced at his watch on the floor next to the bed.

We don't have to go anywhere just yet, do we? he asked, and turned towards me. He pulled me close.

I shook my head.

What does it mean, he breathed, his voice in my ear, his body against mine, his cock hard, only the white sheets between us now, what does it mean when you shake your head, does it mean you don't want to [a jarring laugh], or does it mean that we don't have to go anywhere just yet?


I don't know how many times I lay on his cold blue-tiled bathroom floor, or felt sick and threw up. Was it the first morning or the next one or the one after? I get the mornings mixed up. He knocked on the door and asked me what I was doing, locked in the bathroom for so long.

What the fuck are you doing in there?

And I replied: I'm putting on my make-up.


Because today – my second day in Paris – can't compare with the day before. It's nine in the morning, or maybe ten. K and I get into the red jeep, he behind the wheel, I next to him, almost as if we're a couple, to drive to the studio, the bunker, but before all that, he buys sandwiches and coffee from a café around the corner, we eat in the car, I can't eat all of mine, white bread with cheese and ham, I feel sick again, the ham is thick and pink, edged with a fatty rind. I wrap it up again and place it in my lap.

Now we'll go to your hotel so you can get changed, K says, looking straight ahead. He's wound his window down. He's smoking.

The hotel? *My* hotel?

So you know where it is?

Of course I know.

I'm still wearing the short dress I borrowed from the translator girl. Over that a white windbreaker I've borrowed from K.


We were in his apartment, on our way out, and he'd said: You look sexier in my jacket than in that prim and proper coat of yours.

Okay, I said, and drew the windbreaker around me.

And leave your goddamn woolly hat here, he said, pointing at my red hat on top of my neatly folded blue coat on the chair. You can't go around in Paris wearing a fucking woolly hat.


He starts the jeep, presses a button on the cassette player.

Jimi Hendrix, 'The Wind Cries Mary'.

You like that album a lot, I mumble.

He doesn't reply, lights another cigarette.

It's quite a way to the hotel, too far to walk from his apartment, too far to walk from anywhere, I try to follow where he's going but give up after a short while, he drives fast, turns left, turns right, I glance at the half-eaten sandwich wrapped in paper and think back to when Mamma read 'Hansel and Gretel' to me when I was little. Hansel and Gretel got lost too, because the trail of breadcrumbs Hansel had scattered along the path in the woods in order to find his way home was pecked up by birds.

If things go well today, K says, if all goes well, if you don't go wandering off on your own, crying the whole time, acting like an ungrateful little bitch, if you do as I say, as I suggest you do, then this is just the beginning. French *Vogue* wants to see you. That can change your life, okay? I mean, if they like you, we can start shooting later this week. But only if . . . He turns up the volume on the cassette player, lights another cigarette, almost collides with another car, shouts, *fuck, fuck, fuck*, the thing is, he says, you have to understand, he says, that all the good things, all the nice things, all the beautiful things, will only happen if you don't fuck it all up.

He brakes hard outside my hotel.

Hurry up – he waves me out of the jeep.

I have to call my mother, I tell him.

I open the car door and step out on to the pavement.

Give her my regards, he says, yawning.

I put the sandwich in my pocket.

On second thoughts, don't, he says, looking at his watch. Don't call her. There's no time.

But I promised her, I say, I promised I'd call her.

The manageress sits half asleep on a chair in a small booth at the back of the reception area. A cat stretches out on the desk, the other cats are lying or sitting on the floor and on the stairs. The cat on the desk miaows as I approach, as if it were a watchdog, such a loud miaow that the elderly woman jumps, rubs her eyes and gets to her feet.

She hobbles over and pats the cat, which continues to miaow and arch its back until she tells it to stop.

You, she says, fixing me in her gaze.

She looks almost astonished, as if she's seen a ghost.

I smile.

You, she says again.

She scrutinizes me (at least that's what it feels like), my messed-up hair, the oversized windbreaker, the short, borrowed dress, my black tights.

You, she says for the third time, and then, in a low voice, as if we must be careful in case someone hears us: *Where have you been?*

She speaks in French, but I understand what she's saying, it's not hard. I reply in English that I've stayed the night with a friend, a girlfriend, thinking of the translator girl as I speak, picturing the apartment she shares with Mia, the untidy bathroom, the cold baguette, imagining having slept there, on the sofa, or in the bed next to the translator girl.

The woman shakes her head. Your mother has been calling.

I know, I say.

We're speaking different languages, yet we understand each other without difficulty, as if some great dark language common to us both is at work beneath the words we speak.

I'll call her now, I say.

The manageress nods, her expression still quite as astonished.

She rang once, then rang again, and then again. You've been gone all night, the whole night. The woman now steps out from behind the desk, steps towards me, steps past me to the door,

opens it and looks out. She sees K standing on the pavement in his shirtsleeves, smoking.

She closes the door, steps back behind the desk, takes the key from the mahogany pigeonhole and presses it into my palm.

You must look after yourself, she says, then pats my head. She neatens my hair like I am a little girl on my way to school, tucks a strand behind my ear.

I'm in a hurry, I tell her, and back away.

I resist the urge to let myself be held.

The sixteen-year-old girl dials her mother's New York number. Not the office number. Not the home number. But the *secret* number. The number the girl has been told not to call because — and this is her mother's explanation — the secret line must never be engaged in case someone tries to calls with an important message. But this is important. It's not a message exactly, but it's important. *Mamma, I was supposed to call you last night at ten and I didn't. Have you been waiting? Were you scared?* I don't think it occurred to me that she might have been scared. It occurred to me that she was probably angry. For not being at the hotel when I was supposed to be. For not keeping to our agreement. For not abiding by my ten o'clock curfew. For getting lost in the middle of the night. For sleeping with K. For asking K for more. Don't stop, I said, don't stop. For being born with this desire. For being sick over and over again in a grown-up man's apartment. It's morning in Paris and the middle of the night in New York. Mamma picks up right away.

Hello?
    Mamma's hello is impossible to decipher.

It's me.

Where have you been?

I was . . . I slept at a friend's house, a girl.

A girl?

Yes, a girl I met yesterday.

Why didn't you call me? Why weren't you in your room? We had an agreement!

I was going to call you, I promise, only the phone at my friend's house didn't work, and then it got late, and then I didn't want to wake you, even though I know I'm probably waking you now, because it's the middle of the night there.

I called and called, I think she probably says then, but I can barely hear her voice, either it's a bad connection or she's not talking into the receiver, or perhaps she's so angry she can't speak clearly. I called you at ten o'clock, she says, the time we agreed.

*Ever since I gave birth to you, I've been afraid of losing you.*

Where are you now?

I'm at the hotel.

But you weren't at the hotel at ten o'clock last night?

But Mamma —

No, I don't want to hear it.

I know, but listen to me, please.

You broke our agreement.
I didn't brea–
We had an agreement.
But Mamma –
You broke our agreement.
But Mamma (my voice must not crack), I want to go home!

I want to go home.

I want to go home. Those were the words I wanted to say, tried to say, the words *I remember saying*, but I don't think they were the words that came out of my mouth at that moment in January 1983.

I think what came out was: *But Mamma, I have to go now, I have to hang up.*

Soon I'll be taking off most of my clothes and putting on a white dressing gown. The dressing gown will be tied at the waist and pulled down over my upper arms to expose my neck and shoulders. It's the long earrings you're meant to notice when you open the magazine and see the picture.

Claude screams at the girl (the one in a hat and a coat) who appeared in the doorway and was about to step into the studio – screams that she has a face like a cunt.

The girl is not me, and today is not yesterday.

*You should be ashamed of yourself,* Claude yells, as if the girl's face offends something very tender inside him. He throws his arms in the air, *shame, shame on you.* The girl starts weeping. Shame on you for coming to work with a face like a cunt. Covered in zits, like a schoolgirl. K looks across at Claude. *What's going on?* The music continues, but several people who've been moving about the studio stop and turn their heads in the direction of the door. K puts his camera down, crosses the floor and tells Claude to calm down. He looks at the girl. Takes her face in his hands, turns it this way and that.

Claude is right, he says calmly, I can't photograph you like this, go home and don't come back until you're blemish-free, this isn't something we can magic away with make-up and lights.


And soon it's my turn to be photographed.

I've been made up to look like I'm not wearing make-up.

Untouched, says the make-up artist, pleased with his work. That's the trick, he says. He looks at my face in the mirror, his voice almost a whisper now: This – the untouched, the unblemished, the unspoiled look – is what has made K such a sought-after photographer. To hell with all the cosmetic nonsense, the dramatic lighting, the striking angles.

I sit down on the tall chair, under the light of the lamps, pull the dressing gown down over my shoulders.

I'm ready.

K comes towards me, smiling.

I feel a nip in the earlobe as I fasten one of the earrings.

The elms in Torshovparken have dropped their pellets. Elm seeds lie piled up along the paths and under the trees, strewn about the grassy slopes. The heaps of seeds are nothing to be concerned about, a dendrologist notes in a newspaper interview. The elms are extra fertile, that's all.

Mamma and I sit beside each other on a bench in the park. Normally she lives in Massachusetts, but now she's come home to Norway for a few weeks. I've brought cinnamon rolls. She tells me about all the things she wants to do now that the world might be opening up, the parts she's agreed to play, the trips she's planned. Why put things off? she says. When you're over eighty, it's stupid to wait. She takes a cinnamon roll.
 My neighbour baked them, I tell her.
 This is the best cinnamon roll I've tasted in all my life, she says.
 Mamma is ready for spring, wearing a lovely lilac dress, a white knitted jacket and knee- length boots. I've placed myself at the edge of the other end of the bench, making sure there's as much distance as possible between us, huddling in a thin black coat and a white woolly hat.

Has your hair finally grown long now? she asks.
Yes.
Can I see?
I shake my head.
Can't you just take off your hat and show me? she says.
I don't want to take off my hat, I say, it's freezing out.
It's not freezing, she laughs, it's almost summery.
I sigh.
How's the writing going? she asks.
It's fine.
Are you writing about that time in Paris?
Yes.
And then, abruptly: But how do you know if you're remembering things correctly?
Oh, Mamma, I don't know.

I don't say anything about the forgetfulness. A splash of white paint where the faces should be. I don't say anything about the drinking either. *Living with alcohol is living with death close at hand*, Duras wrote. Mamma and I don't talk about all that. Cautiously we keep each other's company.

Mamma flies back over the ocean again to her spouse and the labyrinthine house in Massachusetts. I carry on ordering groceries that are delivered to her door.

*Bread*
*Rice*
*Shampoo that smells nice*
*Spaghetti*

I'd like to ask her – now that she's been vaccinated, and after the long periods of lockdowns and reopenings – if she's sending me her grocery lists for her benefit or mine. We're never not thinking of each other. She sends me her lists, I place her orders, the items are delivered. The bread. The rice. The shampoo. The everyday we longed for. Once, not long ago on the phone, she told me (by accident) that she'd been to the supermarket.

I said: But Mamma, are you okay with that now – going to the supermarket, I mean? Do you feel safe?

She went quiet.

When I was a child, and then later when I wasn't a child exactly, when I was sixteen, everyone commented on my mother's beauty. I remember K saying something about her eyes, her lips, her vulnerability, as we lay together with the window open to the street below.

What I like most about her, I told him then, is her laughter. I'd do anything just to make her laugh.

*

And now (on the phone) she laughed.

I hadn't even tried to make her laugh, and she laughed.

She laughed and laughed in that big, lonely house in Massachusetts.

No, no, I didn't actually *go* to the supermarket, she said, of course I didn't, not *properly*, I just popped in to buy a hairbrush and a couple of newspapers – a hairbrush, because the one I've had since before the pandemic is lost, I don't know where on earth it is, but all of a sudden one day it was gone and nowhere to be found – but the point is, and there *is* a point . . . are you listening to me? The point is, my darling, that I absolutely do *not* feel safe, not at all, and in fact I'd really like it . . . if you're still able and can spare the time . . . if I could carry on sending you my lists so that you can order my groceries, the way we've been doing.

And as if to make sure there would be no further misunderstanding, she sent (faxed) me a new grocery list immediately after we had hung up:

*Milk*
*Coffee*
*White ribbon (for gift-wrapping)*
*Cheese*

At the bottom of the page she'd drawn a self-portrait – at least I think it was a self-portrait – depicting a girl with long hair and freckles. The girl was sitting at a window with her knees drawn up under her chin. Through the window I could make out a flourishing garden and a big maple tree.

And again. It was only the one picture that got into the magazine, but I remember him clicking away. I don't know how long I sat on the tall chair, under the lights with my shoulders bare, my long earrings. Minutes, hours. We practise, we start again, we're never done. One more time, he said, don't move. He stepped towards me, opened and closed his mouth and gestured for me to do the same. I opened and closed my mouth. Good, he said. Now again. And again. That night, or the night after, in his apartment, wrapped in white sheets, always the same, he said that if I wanted to look beautiful in photographs, which of course I did, then I was going to have to learn to goddamn relax. *Fuck*, he said. I remember only bits of what he said. Sometimes he said *fuck* meaning fuck, and other times he said *fuck* meaning goddammit. Sometimes he probably meant both. When you tense up, he said, your face will tense up too, especially around the mouth and lips. A beautiful woman with tight lips is not beautiful. A sixteen-year-old with tight lips. *Fuck*. Never. And again. He smiled, opened and closed his mouth. We're lying in the white sheets. I've taken my clothes off. Long, strong legs, long neck, broad brow, big mouth, round breasts that aren't fully developed yet. The grown-up woman's body is taking its time. I didn't get my period until I was fifteen. And then it disappeared after Paris. And the exact shape of my breasts as they were then – the winter of 1983 – has only been witnessed by K.

In the white sheets, always the same, he kisses me again. Again. And again. His kisses are wet, he talks and kisses, and talks again, and after a while there's no difference between words and kisses. He pulls me towards him, holds me tighter than the night before, tighter than the night before that, as if we don't have much time, as if I'm going to dissolve and vanish if he lets go of me. His hair, as long or maybe slightly longer than mine, falls into my face, a thousand threads. He shoves a pillow under my behind so he can hold me even tighter, even closer. He laughs, and runs his fingers through my hair.

Every time I feel the nausea welling up in me, I get up and run to the bathroom and throw up.

Every time he comes, he closes his eyes and I open mine.
    Every time he sleeps, he closes his eyes and I open mine.

\*

I wind the white sheet around me and sit up in bed. I know. I know it's rude to look at him while he's sleeping. Rude to indulge myself in such a way, night after night after night. I'm not a man. I'm not an adult. It's rude, it's thrilling. I pull the covers away. His naked almost forty-five-year-old body has little tufts of hair here and there. When he sleeps, age already has him in its grasp. He's so unprotected. His long, wispy curls. Maybe I should cut them off. There's no desire here now. I don't want him. Sleep has taken all of it. His body bulges and shrivels. Unlike mine. I am sixteen years old. He can't hear me giggle. He is fast asleep. His body resembles fruit, overripe apples in a bowl, on the table beneath the window.

Often when he wakes, I'll be lying down again. He draws me towards him. He whispers something in my ear. He tells me about his family. His wife. (He's had several.) His sons. His house by the sea. He says: I'd like you to meet my eldest son. Come over, spend the weekend. My son's only a couple of years older than you. I'm sure you'd hit it off. Absolutely. You and him.

In the red jeep, the second day, the third day, the fourth day, the music turned all the way up. He smokes. He yells. I tell him I want to go home. *Home* home. To New York. I don't want to be here any more.

What about the photo shoot, he yells, for French *Vogue*?

We can do it some other time, I mumble.

Jesus Christ, he says. It's not something we can do some other time, it doesn't work that way, it's a big fucking deal. *Oh, I do apologize* if staying in Paris a few days longer is too much of an inconvenience for Her Highness!

I'm sorry.

Sorry, sorry, he mimics, sorry, sorry, sorry.

I start crying.

And here we go again, he says, swerving to avoid a pedestrian, lighting another cigarette. *Crybaby*, he says. The little princess wants to go home to her mother. Neurotic little bitch. I wish I'd never met you.

I don't remember one day from another. I don't remember how many days I was there, in Paris, in January 1983, perhaps five or seven. I don't know. Many years later, when I had children of my own and the children were sick, days and nights would all blur into one. Everything changes when a fever is coming on, the crimson cheeks, the dreadful exhaustion. The laughter gone. When a child is sick, time moves at a different speed. There's no way of distinguishing Monday and Thursday, four in the afternoon and two in the morning, only that two in the morning is slightly grimmer.

\*

After the stranger, the nightwalker – the man in the red scarf – walked me to K's apartment, I couldn't keep track of hours and days.

I showed him the scrap of paper I had in my pocket, the one with K's address on it, and he walked me the whole way there.

He talked and talked in French. He knew the city. All I had to do was follow.

*Voilà*, he said when at last we stopped outside K's building in the street that might have been rue des Anglais. He stood between two lamp posts, his face illuminated, almost ghostly white, the red scarf around his neck, as he waited for me to thank him. It was late, it was the middle of the night, he deserved to be thanked, he said, for walking me all the way.

Actually, I really want to find my hotel, I said then in a blend of French and English, very quietly but loud enough for him to hear. And then I said: But I can't remember the address, I can't remember what the hotel is called.

For God's sake, he said. Are you totally stupid?

No, I said, I'm not.

But you can't just wander the streets looking for a hotel when you don't know the name or the address.

He stood there with his red scarf on, between the two lamp posts, and every time he spoke, frosty breath puffed from his mouth.

No, he said, I can't help you with that. I've brought you here, all the way to the door, that's quite enough.

I'm writing this in the evening, before a new, quiet night. I hope for rain. Pouring rain. Buckets of rain. At night I lie awake and pray for the sound of wind or rain or voices in the courtyard, anything that's audible.

One night my husband finds a book on his phone and says out loud into the darkness of the room: *The good rain knows when to fall*, and begins to read from an old Chinese poem.

Over and over, he reads the lines.

You wanted rain, he says gently, so now I'll read to you until you fall asleep. And then he whispers: *The green commences tomorrow in the afternoon.*


Afternoon is the best time of the day. A few months ago, afternoon was the worst time of the day. There's no system. I have no sway over it. The green park, the children, the dogs. I walk along Agathe Grøndahls Street, cross over Johan Svendsens Street, past Edmund Neuperts Street to Jolly Kramer-Johansens Street. Many of Torshov's streets are named after composers, several of whom are women. The city streets, up and down the urban landscape, remind me of long arms holding us tightly. Not in an unfriendly way. No, with care. The kind of care exhibited by someone who's seen it all, experienced it all, and who, in addition, has had the advantage of being both living and dead. When the composer Agathe Backer Grøndahl died in June 1907, Edvard Grieg, who passed away only three months later, wrote: *Thus ended this beautiful life. Beautiful in its noble pessimism and in all its suffering. No artist soul has ever walked on purer paths.*

It's unclear to me what Grieg meant by *Beautiful in its noble pessimism and in all its suffering*, or how such dispositions can in any way be related to *purer* paths, but maybe he meant *truer* rather than *purer*? True and pure are often confused. One day, not long ago, I came upon a video clip on the Internet: a woman in a blue dress, an unknown, is seated at a grand piano playing Agathe Backer Grøndahl's 'Song of the Roses' in what looks to be an empty church somewhere in the world, so quietly, and with such restraint, that it feels like solace.


Agathe Grøndahls Street stretches from Vogts Street along the northern end of Torshovparken and Torshovdalen, the park and the valley, passing the wide steps up to the first park, the avenue of trees, and the bandstand. I'm on my way, not to the park, but to the valley. People not familiar with the neighbourhood will often get the two almost identically named green areas mixed up; they agree to meet up in either Torshovparken, called the park, or Torshovdalen, called the valley, and end up missing each other: while A waits in the park, B waits in the valley. Eva and I have agreed to meet by the large bronze doll's head in the valley. I have with me two large paper cups and a Thermos.

Walking along the streets of Torshov today, with the dog in tow, and on my way to meet Eva, I can't understand what has hurt me so terribly until now.

Eva is an ice swimmer.
All through the winter she swims in freezing lakes, ponds, rivers.
All through spring, summer and autumn too, for that matter – but then it's not ice swimming, just swimming.
Sometimes she asks if I want to come with her, she knows a spot where there are hardly any people, and where it's easy to keep your distance if anyone happens to show up at the same time.
She says that swimming in cold water calms restlessness.
I'm not restless, I tell her.
Yes, you are, it's so obvious.

Once, my father said something I rather wish he hadn't. He said: Listen, my heart, you'll survive, but you have a shadow-sister who won't, who's frightened and who'll go to pieces if anyone so much as breathes on her. She needs you.

He leaned towards me and said:

Some people survive, some people don't.

I think my father made these remarks so I'd pull myself together, stop missing school, not fall by the wayside. The conversation unfolded in his living room, in his small apartment on Karlaplan in Stockholm. He knew nothing about the days in Paris. I've no idea what he would have said if I'd told him. Probably not very much. It was a different time. We sat on either side of the coffee table, he in the rust-red armchair, I on the green sofa. The refreshments were light: a bottle of mineral water and a glass for each of us. We weren't alone for very long. Twenty minutes or so after I'd arrived, another three daughters appeared, my real-life sisters, and sat down next to me.

Later I found myself thinking he could have been gentler. *Shadow-sister. Survive. Fall by the wayside.* Maybe I wasn't a child any more – I've wondered about that in connection with this story, wondered whether I was still a child when I was sixteen. I was certainly *his* child, in the sense that whenever he said something about who I was, or who he thought I was, I took it very seriously, and once he'd said what he said there was nothing I could do one way or the other; the story about us, my shadow-sister and me, *you and me*, was a given, or at least that's how it seemed.


Listen, Pappa said, some people survive, some people don't, and even if his words weren't as harsh as I remember them, it was their harshness – their irrefutability – that stayed with me.


Eva comes toward me, tall and pale, dark blue eyes. A delicate black silk dress, a big white sweater on top. An old blue handbag we share, sometimes it's mine, sometimes hers. We meet at the large bronze doll's head in the midst of all the green. She has also brought paper cups and a Thermos.

Now we have four cups and a Thermos each, she says. She's been swimming.

I ask where.

She replies.

I ask who else was there.

She replies.

I ask if she's got a woolly hat with her in her handbag.

She replies.

I ask if she's going to put it on so as not to catch cold.

She replies.

Her hair is damp and salty. The sun is out.

She pours us both some coffee. Steam rises from our cups.

I look over at her and our eyes meet.

She's sixteen, she's seventeen, she's nearly eighteen years old, and there's so much I want to tell her, so much I want to put across, about everyone who came before us, about the streets being like long arms, about restlessness, about the large bronze doll's head we're leaning against, holding our coffee cups, about woolly hats and winter, about acceptance and devotion, but it's not what she needs from me. A gust of wind picks up. It takes hold of her hair, our Thermoses, the paper cups we drink from, snaps at the hem of her dress. It all reminds her of something, but she doesn't say what. She looks out across the green valley, smiling.

The storm has died down in New York and the day is almost spring-like, marking the transition from February to March 1983. I walk the short distance from school to K's building. I take the elevator up to his floor. I walk down the long corridor to his studio. I knock, open the door cautiously and call out.

Hello, anyone here?

Claude, not K, is sitting on a chair facing the door, the back of his head towards the mirrored wall. I meet his gaze the moment I've closed the door behind me and stepped into the studio.

You, he says.

Is K here? I say.

K will be back soon, he says.

He asked me to come, I say.

I know, he says.

The chair is the kind that can go up and down and spin round and round, and Claude, who's adjusted it so that he sits high, begins to spin.

Why don't you come over here and sit with me? he says.

I glance back at the door I've only just closed behind me.

Perhaps I'm thinking: I can leave.

He won't run after me.

It's only a few steps, leave.

It's only a few steps, leave, go back out the door.

It's only a few steps, leave, go back through the door and get out.


I move a few steps, but in the wrong direction, I stand in front of the spinning chair, positioning myself in such a way that Claude can reach out and pull me towards him, which he does.

Sit down here, he says and pats his knee.

He lets go of me and spins again a couple of times. If you don't want to, he says, then you don't want to.

He breaks the spin with his leg, pulls me towards him, and I sit astride him.

That's the way, he says, and we spin a couple of times locked in this position.

He brakes again.

You're pretty, he says, not exceptionally pretty, not beautiful like the other girls, you know that, but pretty.

Shall I say thank you?

Thank you, I say.

He smiles.

Where is K? I ask.

He'll be here, but not yet. Tonight, maybe.

*

Then he goes quiet. I do too. He holds me firmly with one hand and unbuttons my white shirt with the other. He pulls my bra down and pinches a nipple with his knobbly fingers. Then he leans forward, takes my breast in his mouth and starts sucking on it.

His hand moves now here, now there – pinching, stroking, squeezing, jabbing.

I don't know how long we're locked like this. I look at us in the mirror, don't look away, don't move, you're going to remember this for the rest of your life: the girl in the unbuttoned white shirt, sitting astride the old man as he sucks her breasts, first one, then the other. He doesn't kiss her, doesn't caress, doesn't hit her. He moves one hand over her body, softly, cautiously, anxiously perhaps, as if he were climbing a mountain and has to be careful not to fall – hungry, broken, horny.

Locked for how long?

When the studio door, which I had closed behind me, opens, Maxine appears. It takes maybe three seconds. One second to see, two seconds to not believe what you're seeing, three seconds to confirm that what you're seeing is in fact the thing you didn't believe you saw. First a glaring light. Then the make-up mirrors. It's the make-up mirrors I remember best. The make-up mirrors in the Paris studio, the make-up mirrors in the New York studio. They're mounted so that you can see yourself and everyone else from all different angles. In 1983 Maxine was fifty-five years old, the same age as I am today. When reimagining this scene between the girl who used to be me and the man I'm calling Claude, I've tried to understand what it might have been like to be Maxine. I mean — at that exact moment in time.

*What did you see, Maxine?*

The old man with his soft body — as soft as a mushroom, as soft as a baby's eager mouth, as soft as October leaves heavy with rain — sitting on the swivel chair with the girl on his lap. The girl straddles him so all you see are parts of him. The girl's feet dangle. You notice her knee-high boots, but it's *his* feet, *his* polished black shoes solidly planted on the floor, that you can't seem to forget when this comes to mind. In the mirror — the mirrors — you can see his stooped back, his lowered head, you can't see his mouth, clamped around her breast. The girl is naked from the waist up. Her white men's shirt has been pulled down and lies bunched around her waist. She sits on his lap, astride him, her feet suspended. Her head above his, facing the door — the door you opened to come in. The girl catches and tries to hold you with her eyes. You don't want to look at her. You look away.

I'm so sorry, Maxine says, her voice terse, I came for K, but I can see he's not here.

She wheels around, goes back out and shuts the door behind her.

While writing this, I've been thinking about the chain of events and whether one thing inevitably will cause another, and another, and so on. Or if everything is simply an arbitrary selection of moments in time. If I'd started somewhere else, would this story have been a different one altogether? I've been wondering whether K knew that Claude was waiting for me in his studio that day, whether K had told him I was coming over and that I was his for the taking. Or did K tell the truth when he called me the following day to say he was sorry, one of his sons had needed to be picked up at school, he'd tried to reach me to arrange another time?


Was Claude there when you came over?
    Yes, but you knew that didn't you?
    No. Why? Did he say something?
    He said you weren't there.
    Did anything happen?
    No. I left when I realized you were gone, and told him to say hello if he ran into you.


K phoned several times after the thing with Claude. Then one day he stopped calling. It was over.

Spring is approaching, though it's still chilly, four, five degrees Celsuis, it doesn't *feel* like spring. Besides, it's raining. Day after day after day. On 8 March 1983, Ronald Reagan delivers one of his most famous speeches to an audience of evangelical Christians in Orlando, Florida, likening the Soviet Union to what he calls the evil empire. *Yes, let us pray for the salvation of all of those who live in that totalitarian darkness – pray they will discover the joy of knowing God. But until they do, let us be aware that while they preach the supremacy of the State, declare its omnipotence over individual man, and predict its eventual domination of all peoples on the earth* . . . It must have been right after, on a Wednesday or a Thursday, that I opened the door to this part of the building for the last time. I'm not here to see K. I'm here to see Maxine. She's asked me to come. Go to school first, she said on the phone, as if she were my mother, then stop by afterwards.

Why did I put on my pink-and-white striped dress this morning, the oversized leather jacket and knee-high boots? I ditched the red woolly hat, ditched hats altogether, and decided on a big white umbrella that I shook and folded before stepping into the elevator. K once told me that he fell in love with my smile when we met that first time in this elevator. *You smiled at me and*

*I fell in love.* I wore the same dress then as today, the same leather jacket too.

For a while people said:

He *discovered* you.

You were *discovered* in an elevator.

I don't think it's true that I smiled. I rarely smile. Mamma always says: You never smile any more, it can't hurt to smile once in a while.

In the elevator going up, I pull at the edges of my dress, fidget with the thin spaghetti straps. The dress is too tight around my chest, it's too pink, too girlish alongside the leather jacket, the black tights and knee-length boots. I haven't worn it since that first time in the elevator, when I met

K. I wish I'd picked something else today.

Maxine is at her desk. She's busy writing something on a monogrammed pad. She is exceedingly elegant in a loose-fitting black ensemble that looks unfinished, no matter, she's thrown it on anyway. It's impossible to tell what's front and back — which makes both her and it somehow irresistible. She doesn't acknowledge me when I come in. I take a seat on the sofa and put the umbrella down on the floor.

Still without looking at me, she tells me that she's under the impression that I'm not quite serious about making something of myself.

I interrupt, which doesn't please her. She holds up an impatient hand to shut me up.

But *I am* serious, I manage to get out.

Some would think not, she says.

The thing is, I didn't really want to do it, I offer quietly.

Maxine sighs.

You left Paris. You were careless about your work. I mean, have you no shame? And as for what I witnessed between you and Claude –

I interrupt again:

That wasn't my fault, I insist, nudging the white umbrella with the toe of my boot.

Maxine does the impatient thing with her hand again, taking me in with her gaze.

Perhaps you're under the illusion that all life requires of you is to be a cute sort of girl in a cute dress.

Maxine pauses, as if searching for the right words.

I thought you would have inherited some of your parents' grit . . . I imagined you'd be a girl who knew the difference between right and wrong.

Yes, but . . .

Maxine gets to her feet.

I understand that the conversation is over and do likewise, remembering to pick the white umbrella, still dripping, off the floor.

Now that the two of us are standing face to face, she smooths a hand quickly over my hair before gripping the lapels of my jacket. She sighs, smiles, is about to say one more thing, but decides against it. And with that she nudges me gently out through the door of her office.

The picture K took of me appears in a French fashion magazine in the early summer of 1983. The magazine no longer exists. I remember buying two copies from a newsstand on Columbus Avenue that sold foreign publications; I intended to give a copy to my mother, though I don't think I ever did. I remember cutting the picture out, tucking it between two pages in a white wire-bound notebook. I've moved a number of times since then. And though I've looked high and low, I can't find the notebook or the picture anywhere.

~

The dog and I are on our way to the vet. It's summer now. We walk through Torshovparken and Torshovdalen, walk the whole way. The dog pads along behind me. Now and then I have to tug at the lead to make him move. He stops more than he walks, sniffs everything, barks at other dogs. It's a hassle. Increasingly, I find myself going on walks without him. I tiptoe around the apartment, finding my coat and handbag, hoping he won't notice. Or I pretend I'm going somewhere where he can't join me.

Where are you going?
To a café . . . I'm sorry, no dogs allowed.
But the cafés are all closed.
No, they're not. Everything's opening again now.
It's impossible to lie to a dog.


And now we're on our way to the vet. We're walking the whole way there, through the park and the valley. We're not taking a car, we're not taking the tram.


It's a clacking of limbs every time he gets up from wherever he's lying, on the floor, on the sofa, finding his feet, lumbering towards me, never not knowing when I'm on my way out.


You're too old, I tell him, finding his collar, you bark at everyone, you stop every ten seconds to sniff the tiniest little thing, you tug and pull on your lead.

What the vet says after finishing his examination is: Your dog may collapse at any time due to calcification of his right hip joint, these things can happen on any given day, and without warning.


Our days are like water and filled with fear, says the dog.


At night I lie down and listen to his breathing. If I just let it be, and stop thinking that it's keeping me awake, it's as if I can hear the whole world in every one of his breaths. Breathing in, breathing out. A whole world of voices and sounds in the old dog's heart.
 One night I imagine I can hear *your* voice. Lodged inside me, moving in circles, refusing to die.
 That moist black soil in your heart, you tell me, the ivy running rampant inside your lungs.
 What if I tell you that it'll go away? Or not go away, but there'll less of it, or not less of it, but simply that you'll find a way to hold it all. One morning you'll feel the fear subsiding. Coffee tastes good, the slice of bread tastes good too – and you might even ask for

some more. Another slice of bread with cheese and salted cucumber. The trembling will lessen. The nausea will let up. You'll raise your gaze and see swirls of green in the evening rain.


One day I decide to write to the City of Oslo, to the Parks Department. I've been given the name of someone I think, or imagine, might be responsible for the city's trees.

My question is: How many trees are there in Torshovparken.

Two weeks later I get a reply: *The park contains a registered total of 149 trees: 139 deciduous trees, mostly elm, though also birch, white birch, oak, Norway maple, willow and horse chestnut.*


It's morning, it's afternoon, it's evening. The park and the valley fill up with people walking, sitting, jogging, lying outstretched on the green grass, strolling, exercising, having a picnic with music and food, coffee, beer, wine. Children and grown-ups. Dogs. Trees. *You, you, you.* Yes, you too. I'll never leave you, you say.


You realize, almost as a curiosity, that loneliness hasn't erased you after all.

But where am I supposed to go? I can't remember the name of the hotel, or where it is. The only address I have, because I wrote it down on a scrap of paper, is K's. Blue coat. Red hat. Borrowed dress. I'm sixteen years old and lost. I ask everyone I meet, but no one will help me, except for the man with the red scarf. He walks me all the way there. I notice that his scarf isn't just red but specked with tiny white stars. He lingers between two lamp posts and watches me press the doorbell. The lock buzzes open, I push the door, go inside the pitch-black entrance and climb the staircase. First floor. Second floor. Third floor. K stands in the doorway, waiting for me. The light from his apartment falls on us both.

*GIRL, 1983* contains quotes from the following sources:

Page xxx | The interview with Sharon Olds is from the podcast *On Being* with Krista Tippett. https://onbeing.org.

Page xxx | *What I want to seem I do seem* . . . is from Marguerite Duras, *The Lover*, translated by Barbara Bray (Pantheon Books ,1985).

Page xxx | *Almost as if you were presented with a portrait* . . . is from Anne Carson, 'Variations on the Right to Remain Silent', in *Float: A Collection of Twenty-two Chapbooks Whose Order is Unfixed and Whose Topics are Various* (Alfred A. Knopf, 2016).

Page xxx | *these things happened to me so that I might recount them* is from Annie Ernaux, *Happening*, translated by Tanya Leslie (Seven Stories Press, 2019).

Page xxx | *that untamable, eternal, gut-driven ha-ha* is from Anne Sexton's poem 'The Rowing Endeth', in the collection *The Awful Rowing Toward God* (Houghton Mifflin, 1975).

Page xxx | *I hear the earthworm's song* . . . is from Federico Garcia Lorca: 'New York (Office and Denunciation)', in the collection *Poet in New* York, translated by Greg Simon and Steven F. White (Penguin, 2002).

Page xxx | *Street names must speak to the urban wanderer* . . . is from Walter Benjamin: *Berlin Childhood*, translated by Howard Eiland (The Belknap Press of Harvard University Press, 2006).

Page xxx | The BBC's recording of Virginia Woolf may be accessed at https://www.youtube.com/watch?v=zcbYo4JrMaU.

Page xxx | *plenty of secrets don't require upkeep or lies*, Michael L. Slepian, *The Secret Life of Secrets: How Our Inner Worlds Shape Our Well-being, Relationships, and Who We Are* (Crown, 2022).

Page xxx | *I had a terror since September* . . . is from Emily Dickinson's letter to Thomas Wentworth Higginson, April 1862, published in *The Atlantic*, October 1891.

Page xxx | *'For your own good' is a persuasive argument* . . . is from Janet Frame, *Faces in the Water* (W. H. Allen, 1961).

Page xxx | *But a spear found out the little patch of white* . . . is from Alice Oswald, *Memorial* (Faber & Faber, 2011).

Page xxx | *Ugly angels spoke to me* is from Anne Sexton: 'The Double Image', in *The Complete Poems: Anne Sexton*, First Mariner Books edition (Houghton Mifflin Company, 1999).

Page xxx | The scene rehearsed by the girl and her mother can be found in Ingmar Bergman, *Face to Face: A Film by Ingmar Bergman*, translated by Alan Blair (Pantheon Books, 1976).

Page xxx | *My plan was to never get married* . . . is from Jenny Offill, *Dept. of Speculation* (Alfred A. Knopf, 2014).

Page xxx | *Oh, I hate this house* . . . is from Simone de Beauvoir: *The Second Sex*, translated by Constance Borde and Sheila Malovany-Chevallier (Random House, 2014).

Page xxx | *The storm left scenes of wild beauty* . . . is from Robert D. McFadden in the *New York Times*, 13 February 1983.

Page xxx | *You taught me to exist without gratitude* . . . is from Jane Kenyon, 'Having It Out with Melancholy', in the collection *Constance* (Graywolf Press, 1993).

Page xxx | *as monumental as bronze* . . . is from Jorge Luis Borges: 'Funes the Memorious', translated by James E. Irby, in the collection *Labyrinths* (New Directions, 1962).

Page xxx | *I shall try to keep the following guidelines* . . . The original Swedish-language source is Ingmar Bergman, *Arbetsboken 1955–1974* (Norstedts, 2018).

Page xxx | *harsh rays of light* is from Ingeborg Bachmann, *The Thirtieth Year*, translated by Michael Bullock (Alfred A. Knopf, 1964).

Page xxx | The definitions of *depression* are from the Oxford English Dictionary (online subscription) with the following exceptions: the economy reference is taken from merriam-webster.com; the geology reference is a translation from the online version of NAOB - Det Norske Akademis ordbok på nett, citing a sentence about the saline sea from Aftenposten 1959/553/3/2.

Page xxx | *I have heard whispers from old voices* is from Charles Dickens, *A Tale of Two Cities* (1859).

Page xxx | *Safe we are from all our fears* . . . is a rendering by Martin Aitken of a hymn originally in Swedish by Lina Sandell, '*Tryggare kan ingen vara*', 1855.

Page xxx | *Living with alcohol* . . . is from Marguerite Duras, *Practicalities*, translated by Barbara Gray (Grove Press, 1992).

Page xxx | *This is the everyday we spoke of* is from Marie Howe: 'What the Living Do', in the collection *What the Living Do* (W. W. Norton, 1998).

Page xxx | *The green commences tomorrow in the afternoon* replicates a Norwegian rendering by Georg Johannesen of a line from the poem by Du Fu whose title in Burton Watson's translation is 'Spring Night, Delighting in Rain' (included in Burton Watson, *The Selected Poems of Du Fu* (Columbia University Press, 2002)). The earlier quotation on this page is from the title poem, 'Spring Night, Delighting in Rain', in the Watson translation.

Page xxx | *Thus ended this beautiful life* . . . is from *Edvard Grieg: Diaries, Articles, Speeches*, edited and translated by Finn Benestad and William H. Halverson (Peer Gynt Press, 2001).